The Art of
Graffiti

DISCARD

Other titles in the *Art Scene* series include:

The Art of Animation
The Art of Anime and Manga
The Art of Comics
The Art of Graphic Communication
The Art of Tattoo

The Art of Graffiti

Hal Marcovitz

San Diego, CA

© 2020 ReferencePoint Press, Inc.
Printed in the United States

For more information, contact:
ReferencePoint Press, Inc.
PO Box 27779
San Diego, CA 92198
www.ReferencePointPress.com

ALL RIGHTS RESERVED.
No part of this work covered by the copyright hereon may be reproduced or used in any form or by any means—graphic, electronic, or mechanical, including photocopying, recording, taping, web distribution, or information storage retrieval systems—without the written permission of the publisher.

LIBRARY OF CONGRESS CATALOGING-IN-PUBLICATION DATA

Name: Marcovitz, Hal, author.
Title: The Art of Graffiti/by Hal Marcovitz.
Description: San Diego, CA: ReferencePoint Press, Inc., [2020] | Series: Art Scene | Audience: Grades: 9 to 12. | Includes webography. | Includes bibliographical references and index.
Identifiers: LCCN 2019000767 (print) | LCCN 2019004393 (ebook) | ISBN 9781682825846 (eBook) |ISBN 9781682825839—(hardback)
Subjects: LCSH: Graffiti—Juvenile literature. | Street art—Juvenile literature.
Classification: LCC GT3912 (ebook) | LCC GT3912 .M366 2020 (print) | DDC 751.7/3—dc23
LC record available at https://lccn.loc.gov/2019000767

ONTENT

Introduction Art That Is Hard to Miss	6
Chapter One The History of Graffiti	10
Chapter Two Graffiti Artists of Influence	21
Chapter Three Emerging from the Underground	34
Chapter Four Creating a Following	46
Chapter Five The Messages of Graffiti	56
Source Notes	67
For Further Research	71
Index	73
Picture Credits	79
About the Author	80

INTRODUCTION

Art That Is Hard to Miss

The Los Angeles River is unlike most rivers in that it mostly lacks natural banks composed of dirt and rock. For much of its 52-mile (84 km) path through Southern California, the river flows along concrete banks. These banks were built decades ago to control flooding, but in recent years they have been employed for a much different purpose. Artists have decorated miles of the banks with colorful graffiti (a term that comes from the Italian *graffio*, meaning "a scratch").

Images along the river include cartoonish figures, such as smiling cats, sad-faced clowns, and scowling punk rockers. There are also hundreds of messages rendered in huge, colorful lettering. "The river made [Los Angeles] a force to be reckoned with in the graffiti world,"[1] says graffiti artist Evan Skrederstu.

While Los Angeles is bigger, more populous, and more diverse than many US cities, it shares at least one characteristic with cities as well as some suburbs and small towns across the nation: many outdoor walls, fences, bridge supports, and even subway cars are covered in graffiti, also known as street art. Because graffiti is largely illegal, graffiti artists rarely work in daylight where their craft can be witnessed by anyone who wanders by, including the police. Rather, graffiti artists usually create their art under cover of darkness knowing their work will last only as long as building owners tolerate it. It is not unusual for graffiti to be washed off within hours or days of its creation.

Although graffiti is illegal, many experts agree that it is no less a form of art than oil painting or sculpture. "Most of the opposition to

This elaborate image appears on a concrete wall along the Los Angeles River. Many experts agree that graffiti is a form of art on a par with oil painting or sculpture.

graffiti art is due to its location and bold, unexpected, and unconventional presentation, but its presentation and often illegal location does not necessarily disqualify it as art," says artist George C. Stowers. He adds, "It has form, color, and other base properties as well as an arrangement of these elements into structures that qualify it aesthetically as being art."[2]

Graffiti's Rebellious Spirit

The belief that graffiti should be regarded as legitimate art was not always widely held. Graffiti first started showing up in urban settings more than fifty years ago, scrawled onto exterior walls mostly by inner-city gang members. Eventually, an artistic flare found its way into these gang messages, but it was not until the late 1970s and early 1980s

> "[Graffiti] has form, color, and other base properties as well as an arrangement of these elements into structures that qualify it aesthetically as being art."[2]
>
> —Artist George C. Stowers

that practitioners of graffiti started gaining recognition as legitimate artists. The acceptance of graffiti as a true form of art can be attributed in large degree to the pop music artists of the era. In 1979 the popular rock group Blondie recorded the hit single "The Hardest Part" and subsequently produced a music video showing vocalist Debbie Harry singing and dancing through a set covered floor to ceiling with graffiti. In 1982 early hip-hop artist Malcolm McLaren recorded the song "Buffalo Gal" and produced a video showing dancers performing in front of graffiti-covered walls.

And in 1984 pop superstar Madonna recorded the song "Borderline." In the video produced for the song, Madonna is shown spray-painting graffiti onto statues and expensive cars. At the time, the programming at the new television network MTV was largely devoted to airing music videos, and Madonna's graffiti-enriched video received a lot of airtime. To Madonna's millions of fans, the message was clear: graffiti was both rebellious and hip. Boston University art professor Hugh O'Donnell comments that "the freedom of graffiti, its ability to be anywhere and everywhere, and the sometimes daredevil places it is made give it a romantic edge and powerful exposure."[3]

Warhol and Basquiat

Graffiti's recognition as legitimate art was also growing outside the world of music videos. In 1985 the internationally known artist Andy Warhol collaborated with graffiti artist Jean-Michel Basquiat on an exhibit. Their work did not take the form of graffiti; rather, the two artists worked together on sixteen paintings on canvas for a gallery show. Nevertheless, the Warhol-Basquiat collaboration included works clearly created in the style of outdoor graffiti, featuring bright images and words painted in a stark, slashing style. For Warhol, it was a sharp departure from the art that had made him famous: tongue-in-cheek images that ridiculed elements of American culture such as common household products—most notably soup cans. Commenting on the paintings, *New York Times* art critic Vivien Raynor seemed unimpressed by the graffiti-inspired creations by Warhol and Basquiat. She huffed, "The 16 results . . . are large, bright, messy, full of private jokes and inconclusive."[4]

Years later, art experts have grown much more appreciative of graffiti and the art it has inspired. In 2012 one of the Warhol-Basquiat paintings was displayed in the trendy Gagosian Gallery in London, England. A news release issued by the gallery stated that "the paintings that resulted from [the Warhol-Basquiat] collaboration celebrated their respective aesthetic style and production processes while creating a fresh and unprecedented body of work."[5]

Although graffiti is now widely regarded as art, it is still very much illegal when rendered without permission on exterior walls. Nevertheless, graffiti is as widespread as ever as artists flourish in a medium that has never been hard to miss.

CHAPTER ONE

The History of Graffiti

In 1940 colorful images of bulls, bison, and other animals were discovered on the walls of the Lascaux caves in southwestern France. Archaeologists have determined that the images are about twenty thousand years old, placing their creation in the historical time span known as the Paleolithic era, or the Stone Age. Therefore, the Lascaux images represent what may be among the first efforts by humans to create art. To many experts, the drawings on the Lascaux cave walls, as well as in caves discovered elsewhere on the planet, suggest the roots of modern graffiti can be traced to prehistoric times. "I am not saying that Paleolithic art is exactly like modern graffiti," says University of Alaska zoology professor R. Dale Guthrie.

> The people who used charcoal sticks and red ocher to produce bison murals seem to have worked out of enthusiastic respect for both the hunted and the hunters. But at the same time they drew in ways that were often free, careless, casual, alive [and] gritty. . . . And there is abundant evidence that they did not abstain from modifying, marking over, or scratching out previous art.[6]

In other words, the quickly drawn but often harsh and gritty messages found on urban walls in the twenty-first century are not unlike the images found in the wall art rendered by the artists of the Stone Age.

During the centuries that followed the Stone Age, graffiti often found its way onto walls across the civilized world. In 79 CE, for example, the volcano Mount Vesuvius erupted, leaving the nearby Roman city of Pompeii in ruins. Centuries later, archaeologists uncovered walls that escaped damage by the volcano—and many of those walls were covered with graffiti. "The eruption of Vesuvius preserved graffiti in Pompeii, which includes Latin curses, magic spells, declarations of love, alphabets, political slogans, and famous literary quotes, providing insight into ancient Roman street life,"[7] says Bill Norrington, a geography research associate at the University of California, Santa Barbara.

Graffiti is found elsewhere in the ancient world. The Vikings are believed to have been proficient graffiti artists, leaving their marks on walls wherever they may have invaded. For example,

This image of a bull, found in a cave in Lascaux, France, is thought to be twenty thousand years old and may represent the roots of modern graffiti.

sometime during the ninth century a Viking named Halvdan is believed to have scratched a message onto a wall of the Hagia Sophia, a church in Istanbul, Turkey. Historians have translated the Viking's inscription to read, "Halvdan was here."[8]

Kilroy Was Here, Too

By scratching his name onto a church wall in Turkey, Halvdan may have helped establish the practice by graffiti artists to sign their work—often in signatures that become works of art in themselves. Such was the case with James J. Kilroy, whose signature became known the world over even though he never intended it to happen. During the 1940s, Kilroy was employed as a rivet inspector at a shipyard in Quincy, Massachusetts. At the time,

Art for All Ages

Graffiti is largely regarded as a young person's art, but that is not necessarily true in Lisbon, Portugal. In the Portuguese city, numerous elderly citizens have joined a program known as LATA 65, which teaches participants the techniques of graffiti. Many members of LATA 65 have carried their stencils and spray paints into some of the city's run-down neighborhoods and—with the permission of building owners—have created street art. "LATA 65 is a two-day workshop, four hours each day," says the program's director, Lara Rodrigues. "I've had groups with an average [age] of 74, with seniors of 63 to 93 years old. . . . In a regular workshop, the first day would be totally indoors, with the theoretical-visual part and starting to create . . . the project for the wall, and starting to draw some stencils. On the second day, we cut all the stencils, and after we are all prepared, we go to the street."

Rodrigues says the program has produced many dedicated street artists. LATA 65's first class was held in 2012. It was attended by a retired physician, Luísa Cortesão. Since then, Cortesão has created dozens of stencils and has applied her graffiti to numerous buildings throughout the city. Occasionally, Cortesão brings her grandchildren along. She says, "They love it and sometimes go with me to the street to paint my stencils."

Quoted in Sami Emory, "Meet Portugal's Gang of Graffitiing Grandparents," Vice, June 17, 2015. www.vice.com.

American shipyards were producing battleships, destroyers, submarines, and other vessels for the US Navy to use during World War II. It was Kilroy's job to vouch for the Quincy shipyard's workmanship, ensuring that the rivets were placed properly and would hold the ship together during the stress of combat. To let the sailors know that he personally inspected each rivet, Kilroy signed the words "Kilroy Was Here" across the bulkheads—the metallic walls—of the ships he inspected.

Kilroy's inscription soon became a familiar sight to American soldiers and sailors heading overseas. Many of them adopted the inscription as a humorous yet sarcastic motto—scrawling it themselves on walls in foreign cities and towns they passed through as they waged war. Indeed, in the years following the war, the words "Kilroy Was Here" have been found on walls in France and Germany as well as on islands in the Pacific. Somewhere along the way the inscription became more than a signature—a cartoon of a long-nosed man peering over a wall was added to the inscription. According to author and historian Paul Dickson, "Many graffiti writers made a drawing to accompany the phrase 'Kilroy Was Here,' showing a wide-eyed bald-headed face peering over a fence which hid everything below his nose, except for his fingers, which were shown gripping the top of the fence—Kilroy was the mischievous outsider, staring at, and probably laughing at, the world."[9]

"Cornbread Lives"

Although "Kilroy Was Here" was usually rendered in good fun, by the 1960s the humor had largely gone out of the graffiti found on urban walls. By then, urban gangs had adopted graffiti as a method to mark their streets—using it as a warning to neighboring gangs to stay off their turf. The spread of graffiti onto urban walls was helped by the development of spray paint. Invented in 1949, spray paint soon grew into a major consumer product, providing home owners with a simple method of applying touch-up paint to shutters, door trim, and other objects around the house. By the early 1970s, some 270 million aerosol paint cans were sold annually in the United States.

Still, the scrawled graffiti found on urban walls was hardly meant to be artistic. Using spray paint or felt-tipped markers and grease pencils, gang members usually wrote their names or the names of their gangs on the walls in a sprawling and often jagged penmanship—much to the displeasure of building owners and police, who regarded graffiti as nothing more than vandalism. "I think at first it was more of a vandal-type thing," says Kool Klepto Kidd, a 1960s-era graffiti writer from Philadelphia. "We were just on the subway writing on the advertisements. Whenever there was a little space in there, we would write our names. It was almost like, 'We were here,' like it was our route. We would all write our names, and then we would get on [the subway] again and say, 'Hey this was the train we were on.'"[10] (Kool Klepto Kidd is the street name of the graffiti writer—given the illegal nature of their craft, graffiti makers often prefer to be known by their pseudonyms.)

Philadelphia is the American city regarded as the birthplace of modern graffiti. During the 1960s, it swept quickly across the city as buildings, fences, subway cars, and other exterior surfaces were soon covered in spray-painted messages from gang members. Moreover, the graffiti artist given much of the credit for launching the movement is Daryl McCray, who at the time was known as Cornbread.

He earned the nickname in 1966 when, at the age of twelve, he was incarcerated in a juvenile detention center. He kept pestering the cook to bake cornbread, so everybody in the jail started calling him Cornbread. For years after his release, he painted the nickname on buildings and subway cars all over the city—mostly to impress his girlfriend. In 1971 he hopped a fence at the Phila-

> "I think at first it was more of a vandal-type thing. We were just on the subway writing on the advertisements."[10]
>
> —Kool Klepto Kidd, a 1960s-era graffiti writer from Philadelphia

delphia Zoo and spray-painted "Cornbread Lives" across the rear of an elephant. Years later, McCray explained that a city newspaper had published a story erroneously reporting that he had been killed in a gang fight. "I had to do something to let them . . . know I still exist,"[11] explains McCray.

Stencil Art

While Cornbread and others were marking up buildings across Philadelphia, the practice was also spreading to other cities. In New York City, for example, a seventeen-year-old perpetrator known as Taki 183 spread graffiti with vigor. In 1971 his name became so familiar on the sides of buildings in the city that the *New York Times* assigned a reporter to track him down and learn his story. Taki 183 said his motivation for painting his name across town—including across the base of the Statue of Liberty—was to gain celebrity status. He started writing his

A street artist known as Eyez displays one of the stencils he uses. Many artists now use stencils in order to make the same image over and over.

name on walls following the presidential election of 1968 when he noticed that, long after the election, political advertisements promoting the candidates remained pasted to city walls. He says, "Part of the influence was all the electioneering, that [politicians] could get away with sticking things all over the place. . . . They're putting it everywhere. So why shouldn't I? That was my 16-year-old rationale."[12]

As with Cornbread's work in Philadelphia, Taki 183's scrawls were hardly artistic. But by the late 1970s and early 1980s, a new generation of graffiti artists—many with artistic backgrounds—were drawn to the streets. They aimed to employ graffiti as an outlet for artistic expression. They also brought new techniques to the street, including the process known as stencil art.

Stencil artists use paper or cardboard to create an image—first sketching the image onto the medium, then cutting it out with a knife or scissors. The stencil is then rolled up or folded, taken out to the street, and held against the wall while the artist applies spray paint. Prior to the employment of stencils, street artists had relied on a steady hand to guide the can of spray paint. But now, the lines and form of the image could be worked out in advance.

Many graffiti artists still work in a freehand style, but there is no question that the use of stencils brought a new dimension to street art. In addition to enabling the artist to provide a cleaner, sharper piece of graffiti, use of a stencil also enables the artist to create an image on one street corner, then fold up the stencil, hop on the subway, and create an identical image on another street corner miles away (and, perhaps, even on dozens of street corners in between). "You don't have to spend a lot of time replicating a piece, instead, you can easily replicate anything you want without that much of an effort," says art blogger James Farina. "Yes, it makes sense . . . and the value can definitely be quite astonishing in the end."[13]

The first stencil artist believed to employ the technique on the streets is John Fekner, who created some three hundred

Terms of Art

As with any art form, graffiti has produced its own techniques and terminology. Below are a few important terms.

Bombing: This refers to going all out, meaning completely covering a wall or similar surface with graffiti. In other words, the wall belongs to the bomber, and there is no room for anyone else's graffiti.

Tagging: This is the act of signing the graffiti. Often the tag is the only piece of graffiti an artist will put on the wall. The tag could be a scrawled signature or a symbol chosen by the artist.

Sticker: This is a graffiti-style form of art produced on paper with adhesive backing. Stickers can be plastered onto surfaces rather than painted on.

Bubble letters: This is a style of lettering in which letters have a circular appearance.

Burner: This is a piece of graffiti that is particularly well done—perhaps the top piece of street art in the neighborhood or even the city.

Crazy: This refers to very big—crazy big—pieces of street art. Burners are often crazy.

---

stencil art images across New York City as well as in several European capitals during the late 1970s. Fekner used stencil art to create graffiti, but the images were far from artistic. Mostly he used stencils to create big, bold lettering that made political statements, such as decrying urban blight or challenging politicians to keep their promises. In 1981, though, the French artist Xavier Prou, known as Blek le Rat, started using stencils to paint images of rats across the urban landscape of Paris. Within ten years, Prou painted more than one hundred thousand images of rats on exterior surfaces in Paris. To Prou, the rat symbolized art. (By rearranging the letters in the word *rat*, he suggested, one can form the word *art*.) In the years since he stenciled his first rats onto Parisian walls, Prou has employed stencil art to create many other life-size images of people and animals that have become familiar sights around the city.

Classes and Workshops

Prou's work helped bring international recognition to graffiti as a form of art. Although graffiti remains widely illegal, art experts have recognized its value and avidly promote it as a form of expression, especially for young artists. As proof of its legitimacy, some university art programs have seen the value in teaching the techniques of graffiti art. None offer graffiti as a major, but students can take university-level classes to learn how to paint with spray cans and stencils. Boston University's class, known as Site-Specific Art, is one such course. "Graffiti can be art," says Professor Hugh O'Donnell, who teaches the class. "Art is what we call something when it carries significant human symbolic expression."[14]

> "Graffiti can be art. Art is what we call something when it carries significant human symbolic expression."[14]
>
> —Boston University art professor Hugh O'Donnell

Moreover, some high schools and nonprofit groups that promote artistic expression have also sponsored classes in the techniques of graffiti. One school, Seward Park High School in New York City, turned its acre-sized roof over to art students, inviting them to decorate the walled roof enclosure with graffiti.

And in recent years, a number of nonprofit organizations have been established to promote graffiti-style art. Among them are Graffiti HeART in Cleveland, Ohio; Beautify Earth in Santa Monica, California; Off the Wall in Sherman Oaks, California; Urban Artworks in Seattle, Washington; Living Walls in Atlanta, Georgia; and Crush Walls in Denver, Colorado. These groups share similar missions: promoting graffiti as a legitimate form of art, sponsoring workshops for young street artists, and commissioning artists to produce outdoor works of art—painted on surfaces where owners give permission—so that the public may see the art and gain an appreciation for the genre of graffiti. "Artists are people who can use the support to do something positive and create the next renaissance of our planet," says Beautify Earth founder Evan Meyer. "There's millions and millions of sad walls and the world is our canvas."[15]

> "There's millions and millions of sad walls and the world is our canvas."[15]
>
> —Beautify Earth founder Evan Meyer

Murals and Graffiti

When these groups and others find outdoor venues to host graffiti, it is always done with the permission of the property owners. In fact, art painted legally onto exterior walls is a familiar sight in many cities. Known as murals, the artists who create the works are likely to have been commissioned to create the art, meaning they are paid for their talents.

Murals such as this one require more time to create than traditional graffiti.

There are other significant differences between murals and graffiti. For example, the time employed by the artists to create graffiti and murals is usually vastly different. Simple forms of graffiti—the signatures or personal symbols of the artists, known as *tags*—may be applied in no more than a few minutes. Stencil art takes longer, but simple designs can still be applied in short order. A mural, however, may take an artist weeks to design and create. And whereas graffiti is typically applied with a can of spray paint, the paint for a mural is often applied with brushes, requiring several coats.

Still, many experts believe the lines between graffiti and murals have started to blur. Gino Tucillo, a graphic designer from Asheville, North Carolina, says the artistic qualities of graffiti often match those of urban murals. And, he says, both serve the same purpose: to add color and beauty to city neighborhoods. He says, "If it's just random tagging to scar property and identify someone's ego—it's a crime. However, when you happen to walk through some dilapidated back alley and you find a giant, beautiful, sweet face of Yoda staring at you on some old forgotten brick wall and it simply says 'Jedi' next to it, that to me expresses something powerful."[16]

Graffiti has moved far beyond the days of the Lascaux cave artists and Halvdan the Viking; it has evolved into a popular form of modern art. No longer just scratches on the wall, graffiti is a form of art requiring skill with its techniques and a creative spirit among its practitioners. And although the lines are starting to blur between what constitutes a mural and what makes up the typical piece of graffiti, graffiti remains largely illegal—meaning street artists must be willing to risk breaking the law to pursue their passion.

Chapter Two

Graffiti Artists of Influence

Although graffiti is an art form that finds its roots in the urban gang culture of the 1960s, many graffiti artists have emerged as true leaders in their medium—proving that graffiti should be regarded as serious and popular art. Among these leaders is Shepard Fairey, who helped turn images that first appeared on urban walls into popular cultural icons. Keith Haring and Marc Ecko found ways to turn graffiti into successful businesses. Sandra Fabara proved that graffiti is not a males-only medium. Brazilian brothers Gustavo and Otavio Pandolfo have helped ensure graffiti remains a voice of social consciousness. And the British graffiti artist Banksy has won acclaim for work that satirizes modern society even as the artist's identity remains secret—a talent all good graffiti artists can appreciate.

Shepard Fairey and the Posse

Shepard Fairey was a student at the Rhode Island School of Design in 1989 when he discovered stencil and sticker art. Paging through a local newspaper, he came across a photo of a professional wrestler known as Andre the Giant. "I was teaching a friend how to make stencils," says Fairey,

> and I looked for a picture to use in the newspaper, and there just happened to be an ad for wrestling with Andre the Giant and I told him that he should make a stencil of it. He said, "Nah, I'm not making a stencil of that, that's

stupid," but I thought it was funny so I made the stencil and I made a few stickers and the group of guys I was hanging out with always called each other the Posse, so [the sticker] said "Andre the Giant Has A Posse."[17]

Fairey wandered throughout Providence, Rhode Island, the city where the design school is headquartered, plastering the stickers showing the wrestler's gruff expression on exterior walls, telephone poles, bridge supports, and other surfaces. Soon Fairey was approached by friends who asked him for copies of the stickers, which they also plastered on exterior walls. And then strangers approached him—many of them from the Providence skateboard community—asking for Andre the Giant stickers as well. On weekends Fairey and his friends traveled to New York City or Boston, where they continued to paper exterior walls with the wrestler's image. Within weeks, *Andre the Giant Has a Posse* was a familiar image across urban streets in a number of US cities. Says Fairey, "I started to realize that an image in public has this power to be provocative and the more that it's out there, the more important it seems and the more important it seems, the more people want to know what it is."[18]

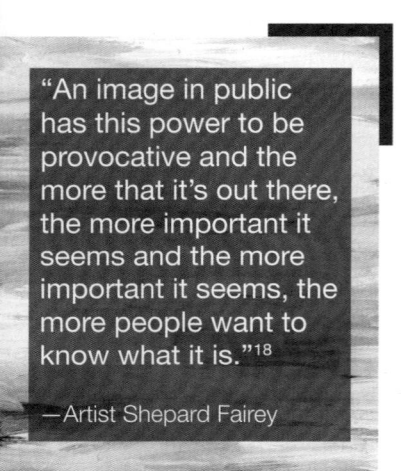

> "An image in public has this power to be provocative and the more that it's out there, the more important it seems and the more important it seems, the more people want to know what it is."[18]
> —Artist Shepard Fairey

Fairey's discovery that a provocative yet artistic image could capture the public's attention marked an important moment in the evolution of graffiti as a form of art. Indeed, for centuries the public had come to recognize important pieces of art, such as Leonardo da Vinci's *Mona Lisa* and Auguste Rodin's bronze sculpture *The Thinker*, as familiar cultural icons. Now, due to street artists like Fairey, images that had started out as graffiti were finding similar recognition.

In the years since creating *Andre the Giant Has a Posse*, Fairey has moved away from illegal graffiti, confining his street art to com-

Shepard Fairey's *Hope* Poster

The graffiti community received a major dose of legitimacy in 2008 when Shepard Fairey's image of Barack Obama became the unofficial logo of the future president's campaign. The artwork featured a red, blue, and white portrait of Obama with "Hope" stenciled under the portrait.

The street artist was an avid supporter of Obama's candidacy. He created the image using stencil art early in the campaign, first printing it as a poster. He sold the poster on Los Angeles streets, and enthusiastic Obama supporters soon plastered the image around the city. As Obama's candidacy gained traction, Fairey's portrait gained widespread recognition. Throughout 2008 Fairey printed about three hundred thousand copies of the poster.

Shortly after Obama's inauguration as president in January 2009, the Smithsonian Institution in Washington, DC, announced that it had acquired the original work of art and that the portrait of the president would be displayed in the museum's National Portrait Gallery. "What I think is so fascinating is the ubiquitous nature," said Carolyn Carr, deputy director of the gallery. "When people think of a portrait of Obama, they think of this image."

Quoted in BBC News, "Gallery Gets Iconic Obama Image," January 8, 2009. http://news.bbc.co.uk.

missioned murals. He also works on canvas, and his paintings have been offered for sale in numerous private galleries. Moreover, many museums have staged exhibits of his work, among them the Smithsonian Institution in Washington, DC; the Los Angeles County Museum of Art; and the Victoria and Albert Museum in London.

Keith Haring's Pop Shop

Keith Haring made his mark as one of the first subway artists — meaning he created much of his work on the sides of subway cars. Haring discovered that many New York City subway cars were equipped with blank black panels along their sides — places where advertisements are to be plastered. Working quickly with white chalk, Haring created graffiti on these black spaces, and he soon found a following among commuters who anxiously awaited the arrival of the cars at subway stations for opportunities to view his newest creations. Between 1980 and 1985, Haring is believed to have drawn more than five thousand images on the sides of New York subway cars.

As Haring moved on to other forms of street art, as well as works on canvas, he maintained the same style as the graffiti

Graffiti artist Keith Haring is famous for his cartoon-style images featuring bold black lines accentuated by bright colors.

that commuters saw on the sides of subway cars. As a young boy growing up near Reading, Pennsylvania, Haring had hoped to become a cartoonist. He never lost his flair for cartooning, drawing his figures as cartoon characters with bold black lines accentuated by bright colors.

In 1986 Haring became one of the first graffiti artists to find commercial potential for his work. He opened a store in New York City—the Pop Shop—where he sold original works on canvas, all painted in the same style as his street art. He also decorated T-shirts, hoodies, baseball caps, and other apparel with his images, making those available to customers. After the store opened, Haring said,

> "I wanted to continue this same sort of communication as with the subway drawings. I wanted to attract the same wide range of people, and I wanted it to be a place where, yes, not only collectors could come, but also kids from the Bronx."[19]
>
> —Artist Keith Haring

> Here's the philosophy behind the Pop Shop: I wanted to continue this same sort of communication as with the subway drawings. I wanted to attract the same wide range of people, and I wanted it to be a place where, yes, not only collectors could come, but also kids from the Bronx. The main point was that we didn't want to produce things that would cheapen the art. In other words, this was still an art statement.[19]

Haring's work dominated subway cars and other public spaces in New York City during the 1980s, but he was unable to carry on his work into the next decade. In 1990 Haring died at the age of thirty-two, a victim of the AIDS epidemic.

Marc Ecko's Billion-Dollar Bomb

Marc Milecofsky created his first graffiti at the age of ten—spray-painting an image of a rhinoceros on a wall at the Lakewood Airport in New Jersey. In fact, Milecofsky created a piece of

Banksy's Mischievous Soul

A few years back, one of Banksy's most familiar graffiti images—a young girl holding a balloon in the shape of a heart—was rendered onto canvas by the artist. In October 2018, Banksy offered the painting for sale at Sotheby's, an esteemed art auction house in London, England. At the Sotheby's auction, *Girl with a Balloon* sold for $1.4 million.

But Banksy never collected the prize—nor, it appeared, did the artist ever intend to collect the money. Moments after the auctioneer concluded the sale, the painting—displayed on a stage at the auction house—started dropping out of its frame. And as it dropped, horrified spectators saw that the painting was being sliced apart by a shredding mechanism hidden inside the frame.

Art experts immediately concluded that shredding the painting was merely a stunt staged by the artist. "I wouldn't put it past Banksy to have staged the whole thing, and I wouldn't put it past him to have pulled this off without anyone being in on it," said New York City art curator R.J. Rushmore.

A day after the auction, Banksy posted a video of the self-destruction of *Girl with a Balloon* on Instagram, prompting suggestions that the mysterious Banksy was actually in the auction room when the stunt was pulled, perhaps even controlling the shredder through a remote device. The fact that Banksy was willing to pass up a $1.4 million payment to pull off the prank suggests that the secretive graffiti artist has never moved beyond the mischievous soul that can be found deep within all street artists.

Quoted in Hilary Clarke, "Who Was in on Banksy's 'Self-Destruct' Art Stunt?," CNN, October 8, 2018. www.cnn.com.

---

graffiti that spanned a distance of no less than 200 feet (61 m). In the world of graffiti, Milecofsky had created a bomb—a piece of art so vast that it dominated the wall, leaving no room for the work of another graffiti artist. In middle school, Milecofsky was sought after by his classmates to decorate their jackets and sweatshirts with hip-hop images they could wear while skateboarding. Milecofsky never intended to make art or fashion design a career. Instead, he entered college as a pharmacy major but spent so much of his spare time creating graffiti and stencil art that by his third year in school he lost interest in a career in pharmacy and dropped out.

After leaving school, Milecofsky's sister Marci suggested he start a business, selling clothes decorated with his art. Milecofsky asked a friend for a loan to start the business. The friend offered him $5,000. Recalls Milecofsky, "He said, 'How many T-shirts can you get printed for this?'"[20] That was in 1993; since then, Ecko Unlimited has grown into a company that employs more than fifteen hundred people, selling $1.5 billion in apparel each year. (Milecofsky's nickname as a young boy was Echo; he slightly changed the spelling to "Ecko," which he then used as his tag while creating graffiti.) The logo for the company is an image of a rhinoceros—not unlike the graffiti bomb Milecofsky painted at the Lakewood Airport.

Now known as Marc Ecko, he remains the chief creative force behind Ecko Unlimited. And the image of the rhinoceros he first drew at the age of ten still dominates a lot of the T-shirts, baseball caps, and hoodies sold by the company, but customers can find other images as well: skateboarders, evil-looking clowns, smiling human skulls, and masked bandits—all familiar images that can very well be found on urban walls decorated with graffiti. The company even sells T-shirts displaying the words "Spray Paint"—an obvious reference to the medium first employed by its founder.

Lady Pink and Empowering Women

Since its earliest days, the graffiti world has been a culture of outlaws—artists forced to work under cover of darkness, always risking arrest. Few teenage girls and young women have been willing to take that risk, but some have stepped forward, carving a place for themselves among graffiti's best-known artists. Perhaps no woman has gained more prominence as a graffiti artist than Sandra Fabara, better known as Lady Pink— the tag she has used since her teenage years as a statement declaring that women can excel at graffiti. Fabara, who grew up in New York City, recalls her initiation into the graffiti world back in the 1980s:

> I had already been writing [graffiti] in junior high school—around the building and around the block. But when I went to the [New York] High School of Art and Design, I met some boys who were doing subway trains and it seemed terribly exciting. That was the thing to do. Everyone seemed to be striving to get to the subway tunnel and yard and actually put it up on a train—with that came admiration. I assumed I could do it too, I think, because the feminist movement was catching up with me. Girls were busy proving we could do anything the guys could do and there was no stopping us. The more we were told we couldn't do something, the more we wanted to do it.[21]

Fabara's style is bright, colorful, and psychedelic. She often displays images of women as the central figures in her work. Since her days creating graffiti on walls and subway cars, Fabara has moved on to works on canvas as well as murals. She performs a lot of commissioned work, decorating the interior and exterior walls of many cafés, restaurants, and theaters in New York City.

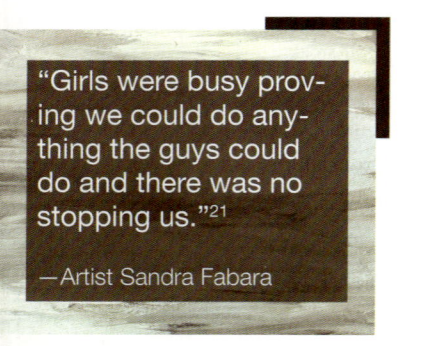

> "Girls were busy proving we could do anything the guys could do and there was no stopping us."[21]
>
> —Artist Sandra Fabara

Commenting on a 2016 gallery show of Fabara's work, art critic Jasmin Hernandez of the website Vice said, "An overall thread of female empowerment and pro-feminist messaging runs cohesively throughout the show. In [her painting] 'Queen Matilda,' the architectural centerpiece is sculpted to personify a woman. This gesture points to the centuries-long role women have held in society as nurturing caregivers and as the backbone of human civilization."[22] *Queen Matilda* displays an image of a woman, composed of bricks, towering over a small village erected atop

28

a mountain. Today, graffiti-inspired art created by the teenager who once spray-painted the sides of subway cars can be found in museums such as the Whitney Museum, the Brooklyn Museum, and the Metropolitan Museum of Art, all in New York City, as well as in the Groninger Museum in the Netherlands.

OSGEMEOS's International Style

Although modern graffiti may have started on the urban streets of Philadelphia and New York City, many international cities have seen the movement grow on their streets as well. Perhaps no graffiti artists have been as instrumental in defining the art form in South America as Brazilians Gustavo and Otavio Pandolfo, twin brothers known as OSGEMEOS. (The Portuguese words *os gêmeos* translate in English as "the twins.")

Brazilian cities have subways, but they are typically heavily guarded against vandalism, so OSGEMEOS and other Brazilian graffiti artists generally stay out of them. Instead, it was the

Graffiti artists Otavio and Gustavo Pandolfo were acclaimed for the images that appeared on the airliner that carried the Brazilian national soccer team to the 2014 World Cup competition.

OSGEMEOS bombings across the sides of buildings that brought the brothers fame as graffiti artists throughout Brazil during the late 1980s and early 1990s. Typically, their art tends to showcase Brazilian folklore or the plight of the country's downtrodden citizens. Most of the characters they paint feature yellow skin—a trait, according to the brothers, that has appeared to both of them in their dreams.

As with many graffiti artists, the brothers have gone on to paint murals and other commissioned works. And their work has also spread beyond South America. In 2017 they were commissioned to paint a two-story-high mural on the side of a building on Fourteenth Street between Sixth and Seventh Avenues in New York City. The mural displays four comical hip-hop characters.

Perhaps no work by OSGEMEOS has earned as much acclaim as their 2014 commission to paint the exterior of the Boeing 737 airliner used to transport Brazil's national soccer team across the country as it competed in the 2014 World Cup. (Brazil was the host country for the international competition.) The twins were invited by Gol, the Brazilian airline that owns the plane, to cover the jet in graffiti-style images.

The brothers covered the plane, nose to tail, with vivid images of large, round yellow and brown faces. According to OSGEMEOS, the job took twelve hundred cans of spray paint. In a joint statement, the artists said the idea of covering the plane with their art appealed to them because of the opportunity for people across Brazil to see their work. They said, "Besides the enormous challenge, for we painted in a totally unconventional medium, the concept of this work is to give unrestricted access to our art. We depicted the Brazilian population with all its varied and colorful ethnicity, bringing this work to the skies and airports in Brazil."[23]

Banksy's Surrealism

Banksy is the graffiti world's most secretive artist. The British artist refuses to provide a real name or appear in public, and no photographs of the artist are known to exist. And yet, by the decade

This surreal image by the British graffiti artist known as Banksy, of a police officer walking a balloon dog, appeared on a wall in Toronto. Despite his international fame, Banksy has kept his true identity secret.

of the 2010s, perhaps no graffiti artist had earned more international acclaim than Banksy. In fact, in 2010 *Time* named Banksy one of the magazine's one hundred most influential people in the world. *Time*'s editors asked Banksy to provide a photo to publish alongside the world leaders on the list—people such as President Barack Obama, Apple Computers founder Steve Jobs, and pop star Lady Gaga. Banksy replied by sending *Time* a photo depicting the artist's head covered by a paper bag.

Despite Banksy's secretive nature, there is no disputing the artist's impact on the world of graffiti as well as the rest of the art world. Banksy is a surrealist—a style of art that dates back to the 1920s, when artists started creating ordinary scenes of people caught up in very unreal circumstances. (The term was first used by French poet Guillaume Apollinaire to describe the genre, which he called "super realism," or "surrealism" for short.)

Banksy's stencil art has featured rats carrying umbrellas, a masked bomber tossing a bouquet of flowers, a policeman walking a dog crafted out of twisted balloons, a panda armed with pistols, a hoodlum stealing one of the five Olympic rings, a young girl getting soaked by rain pouring down from underneath her umbrella, an elephant carrying a missile on its back, and a policeman applying graffiti to a wall using a can of spray paint, among other images. These works have found many followers across the world. According to *Find* magazine, which reports on developments in popular culture,

> Banksy is nothing less than solid. His work tends to be bold and sweeping, his style so distinct that it is difficult to mistake his work for anyone else. Through his incorporation of elements of surrealism, such as a dog shooting a record player, Banksy allows his vision to remain fresh. This quirky side to his artwork is doubtlessly what makes him so attractive to people around the globe. He also makes heavy use of irony, cleverness, wit, and archness.[24]

And while Banksy does collect commissions for murals and has participated in gallery shows, the artist is still very much the outlaw artist. New Banksy images constantly show up on exterior walls along streets in London and other European cities.

Fairey, Haring, Ecko, Fabara, OSGEMEOS, and Banksy proved themselves to be leaders in the graffiti community. They all started out as street artists, tagging and bombing walls and other exterior surfaces. As they moved away from illegal street art, they remained committed to the style of art that propelled their careers—wild and colorful images that can still be found on outdoor surfaces on many city streets, perhaps being made by young graffiti artists waiting for the world to recognize their talents.

Chapter Three

Emerging from the Underground

The art of graffiti has taken many steps forward since it first started showing up on urban walls decades ago. Indeed, graffiti has been transformed from an element of inner-city gang culture into a legitimate art form. Pop music stars have featured graffiti in their music videos, enticing millions of fans with wild and colorful imagery. The styles and materials employed by graffiti artists have been studied and analyzed by art critics, museum curators, and other experts.

But graffiti is still very much illegal. Virtually every city council and state legislature in the United States has adopted antigraffiti laws that regard street art as nothing more than vandalism. Graffiti is classified similarly in Canada, Great Britain, and other countries. Artists caught applying graffiti without permission of the property owner face penalties that could include fines and imprisonment.

Steven Free, a street artist in San Francisco, California, who goes by the tag Girafa, has experienced these penalties firsthand. He has mostly painted graffiti images of giraffes to call attention to the plight of the species. Free does not believe giraffes should be captured in the wild and then displayed in zoos. "I paint giraffes to bring awareness that wild animals don't belong in zoos," he declared. "Just like a painted giraffe doesn't belong on a rooftop, a city wall, or a delivery truck, right?"[25]

Free's outlaw street art days ended abruptly in 2012, when he was arrested by police in nearby San Jose, California, in the act of applying graffiti to a wall. He pleaded guilty to vandalism charges and was placed on probation for three years—meaning that if he was caught creating illegal graffiti again within that time span, he would be forced to finish his sentence in jail. He was also ordered to pay $38,000 to the owner of the building he was spray-painting to compensate the owner for the cost of removing the graffiti.

Controlling Lawbreakers

Hefty fines on graffiti artists—such as the penalty assessed on Free—are imposed by city and state lawmakers to compensate property owners for the high cost of removing paint from exterior walls, fences, subway cars, bridge supports, and other surfaces. According to one study by the US Justice Department, municipal governments as well as private property owners spend at least $12 billion a year removing graffiti from walls and other exterior surfaces. Moreover, in Great Britain authorities estimated in 2018 that British municipalities and private citizens spend $1.26 billion a year removing graffiti. Says Gill Mitchell, a member of the city council for the British community of Brighton and Hove, "As a city council, we work hard to tackle the problem, but sometimes no sooner have we erased a tag then it reappears, with some of these vandals proving to be continual and persistent."[26]

The main reason graffiti is so expensive to remove is simple: it is very difficult to do so. Spray paint dries within hours of its application—in other words, by the time a building owner notices the graffiti during daylight hours, the nighttime artist has long since completed his or her work, and the paint has dried. Cleaning crews typically use chemical solvents, paint scrapers, and power-washing equipment—which blasts the paint with water under high pressure. Another technique is known as sandblasting—shooting sand and air under high pressure at the surface of a wall. And even then, it might not do the job. Porous materials—such as bricks or cinderblocks—often absorb the paint, meaning it may never wash off completely.

Removing unwanted graffiti is difficult and expensive. Despite its growing acceptance as legitimate art, creating graffiti on public or private property is often considered a crime.

Still, city officials believe they have a responsibility to keep their streets free of illegal graffiti. Says the Justice Department study, "Countering graffiti is important for addressing its direct impact on the community's quality of life and perceptions of public safety as well as related public-order problems. The presence of graffiti suggests the government is failing to protect residents and control lawbreakers."[27]

In their fight against graffiti, law enforcement agencies and property owners have found an ally in the construction materials industry, which in recent years has developed coatings for buildings that repel spray paint. Coatings largely composed of the chemical element known as silicon can be applied to the exterior of the building. If, after the building is coated, a graffiti artist comes along and paints the walls, the paint can be washed off easily with no more than a brief pressure washing or even by wiping the paint off with rags. According to Patricia D. Ziegler, the editor of *Coat-*

ings Tech, the trade publication for the coatings industry, "Those who glorify so-called 'urban art' are missing an important point. Graffiti, on property without permission, is not art. It is vandalism."[28]

Tech Aids for Artists

Despite the obstacles—from aggressive law enforcement measures to new graffiti-repellant coatings—graffiti artists continue to pursue their craft. Some technological advancements have even worked in their favor. For example, the computer applications known as Google Earth and Google Street View have been employed by graffiti artists to find exterior walls for their work. By using Google Earth and Google Street View, graffiti artists can scope out neighborhoods as they search for places to create their art without detection.

Another technological advancement employed by street artists is the use of aerial drones. Some graffiti artists use drones to search for new places to apply their art. Drones can also be useful in avoiding detection. By dispatching a drone to hover overhead while the artist works on an exterior surface, the artist can keep an eye on the neighborhood and determine whether security guards or police are in the vicinity. "Drones are being used a lot," says one British graffiti artist, who mostly works on the sides of commuter train cars in London. "It's not uncommon to visit spots regularly for months, watching the trains to see where they stop and for how long—timing them so you know how long you've got."[29]

MuralsDC

Rather than engage in an ongoing battle over graffiti, some city leaders have decided to work with the artists to find legal canvases for their art. These are places where property owners do

> "Those who glorify so-called 'urban art' are missing an important point. Graffiti, on property without permission, is not art. It is vandalism."[28]
>
> —Patricia D. Ziegler, editor of the trade publication Coatings Tech

not object to the art, and residents of the neighborhoods welcome the graffiti as important expressions of modern culture. One city that has declared a truce with its graffiti artists is Washington, DC, which has operated the MuralsDC program since 2007. Each summer, graffiti artists are permitted to paint exterior walls on six or seven buildings selected to participate in the program. By 2019, eighty-five buildings in the city had been decorated with street art under the program.

Since MuralsDC began, the program has had little trouble finding building owners willing to turn their walls over to artists. Many of the MuralsDC buildings are located in gentrified neighborhoods—rehabilitated urban locations that are attracting many Millennial and Generation Z residents. (Millennials were born between the early 1980s and the mid-1990s; they have been followed by Generation Z, young people born between the

Cities around the world are working with artists to find legal canvases for their art. This has been done in Washington, DC, and in Sydney, Australia, where a house displays the work of a street artist named Ox King.

mid-1990s and the mid-2000s.) As Eric A. Vasallo, a screenwriter and social critic, comments,

> Millennials and Gen Z'ers are connecting to this new expression of street art in as many different ways as the unconventional street artists can come up with. For them, the art form seems completely benign as they have no idea of its rough and tumble origins and ties to gangs or turf wars. For them, it's just good, relevant art they get to enjoy for free. Aside from street art's break-all-the-rules appeal, its very accessibility to the masses, no museum hours, lines or entrance fees, is precisely what makes it so easy to connect to. It's that grassroots, talking-to-you-on-your-level that appeals to most anyone. There is more of a connection with the common man and his struggles than mainstream or lofty high-end art.[30]

Art in Good Taste

As Vasallo suggests, programs like MuralsDC realize they have the responsibility to showcase art that is good—and in good taste. Therefore, to be accepted into MuralsDC, graffiti artists must be over the age of eighteen and have no criminal record. Also, they must submit a portfolio of their work to MuralsDC, proving they have the talent to participate. Younger artists are also encouraged to participate, but they must serve as apprentices to the graffiti artists selected to apply their art to the participating buildings.

> "Millennials and Gen Z'ers are connecting to this new expression of street art in as many different ways as the unconventional street artists can come up with. . . . For them, it's just good, relevant art they get to enjoy for free."[30]
>
> —Screenwriter and social critic Eric A. Vasallo

In 2018 Nessar Jahanbin painted a mural depicting mathematician Albert Einstein on the side of a building in the district's Columbia Heights neighborhood. Einstein is known mostly for developing the equation $E=mc^2$. (First published by Einstein in 1905, the equation means energy equals mass times the square of the speed of light. Essentially, the equation explains how the mass of atoms can be converted into energy, which in practice is used to create nuclear reactions that generate electricity or, at the end of World War II, to explode the atomic bomb.)

In fact, Jahanbin's mural depicts Einstein writing his equation—but not with chalk on a blackboard. "It's a famous picture of him at a blackboard," Jahanbin explains. "Instead of the chalk, he's holding a spray can and he's writing graffiti that says $E=mc^2$." Jahanbin says that as he worked on the mural, passersby were generally supportive. He comments, "People are more inspired it seems from the fact that you are doing it. You are actually painting on a wall. That's kind of magical to them."[31]

Jazz Legends and Donkeys

Other cities have developed similar programs. Since 1975 the Baltimore Mural Program has helped artists create some 250 murals across the city. Moreover, after the artists have completed their works, the program applies silicon-based coatings over the murals to prevent them from being painted over by outlaw graffiti artists. In Philadelphia the city's Mural Arts Philadelphia program was established in 1984. Since then it has helped artists create more than sixty public art projects each year. Some of these projects are total bombing efforts—for example, one piece of street art found in the city is located on the side of a two-story home celebrating the life of the late jazz musician John Coltrane, who spent many years as a Philadelphia resident.

Smaller examples of street art can also be found around the city. When the Democratic National Committee held its 2016 convention in Philadelphia to nominate presidential candidate Hillary Clinton, it donated two dozen fiberglass statues of its mascot—a donkey—to Mural Arts Philadelphia. Each statue stood about 4 feet (1.2 m) tall. Street artists responded by

Beyond the Big Cities

When people move out of big cities and into the surrounding suburbs or nearby small towns, many think they will never see graffiti near their new homes; yet that assumption is often wrong. For years public parks and playgrounds and even private properties in suburban communities and small towns have been painted by local graffiti artists. Jeff Goring is a thirty-one-year-old graffiti artist who lives in Durham, Ontario, a small town about 42 miles (68 km) west of Toronto. He has been painting street art on exterior surfaces in Durham since his teenage years. He points out that unlike big cities, small towns and suburban communities rarely sponsor public mural programs, which means graffiti artists have no option other than breaking the law. "What's tough with the culture in this area is kids get hooked on [graffiti] but there's no place for them to do it," he says.

In contrast, some suburban home owners have found the value of their properties increases when attractive, well-done street art comes to their neighborhoods—mostly because young buyers looking for homes believe street art can have a positive influence on culture. That is what home owners have discovered in the community of Newtown, a suburb of Sydney, Australia. "It improves suburbs from a cultural perspective and drives traffic to individual properties. In that way, it's an attribute of the property—and attributes add value," says Sydney real estate broker Greville Pabst. "It also discourages unwanted graffiti, which improves the homes. [Vandals] rarely tag walls with art."

Quoted in Parvaneh Pessian, "Durham Tagged: Graffiti Culture Seeps into the Suburbs," *Oshawa This Week*, May 3, 2012. www.durhamregion.com.

Quoted in Aidan Devine, "Street Art Is Driving Up Home Values in Edgy Inner City Suburbs," *Daily Telegraph*, August 12, 2017. www.news.com.au.

painting the donkeys in vivid colors, some with political messages but others with simple and joyful scenes, such as a horse drawing a carriage through Pennsylvania Dutch country. National political figures visiting the city were enamored with the street art and enjoyed posing for photographs with the donkeys. Elsewhere, the city has even made the buses in its public transit system available to street artists—permitting them to

Statues of donkeys donated to the city of Philadelphia in preparation for hosting the 2016 Democratic National Convention were decorated by local street artists.

paint bright and vivid colors and cartoonish characters along the sides of the vehicles.

In some cities, private property owners have established their own street art programs. In Austin, Texas, the city's Hope Outdoor Gallery was founded in 2011 by graphic artist Andi Scull Cheatham and Vic Ayad, a local housing developer whose company owned a vacant parcel of land in the city that it had intended to use for an apartment building. The concrete foundation was poured for the building, but the project eventually fell through, leaving the large foundation and its wall behind. Once Cheatham noticed graffiti showing up on the wall, she decided that an outdoor murals program would better serve the community. Ayad agreed, and between 2011 and 2018 the property was available to street artists who were invited to paint real murals—not just tags—on the walls. To help inaugurate the Hope Outdoor Gallery, Shepard Fairey painted the first mural. In 2018 the property was sold, temporarily ending the program, but Hope Outdoor Gallery planned to reopen at Carson Creek Ranch, a 58-acre (23 ha) ranch along the Colorado River in Austin, which serves as the venue for music festivals. By 2018 numerous walls were under construction at the ranch, all to be devoted to street art.

New Laws Are a Deterrent

Despite the success of such programs in Baltimore, Philadelphia, Austin, and Washington, DC, some city officials remain unconvinced that graffiti can make a positive addition to urban culture. In 2016 the city council of Bethlehem, Pennsylvania, enacted an ordinance requiring building owners to wash graffiti off their walls within fifteen days of discovering the art. The ordinance was passed not to punish building owners but rather to encourage them to install security cameras around their properties—a measure the council believes would discourage graffiti artists from spray-painting those properties. In addition, the Bethlehem ordinance also established fines of up to $1,000 as well as ninety-day prison sentences for perpetrators caught illegally painting graffiti on properties.

Moreover, in communities that have attempted to reach a truce with street artists, graffiti nevertheless continues to persist on buildings that are not part of their mural projects. Brandon T. Todd, a Washington, DC, city council member, points out that despite his city's public murals program, the Washington public works department spent $447,000 in 2017 to remove more than sixty-six hundred graffiti images from the walls at playgrounds, city squares, and other public places. Private property owners, of course, had to remove graffiti from their own properties at their own expense.

In 2018 Todd proposed raising fines on graffiti artists in Washington from $250 to $2,500. Also, Todd's proposed ordinance would include jail sentences of up to six months for artists caught spray-painting buildings. Todd says he does not want to

Police Use Drones Too

Some graffiti artists have turned to aerial drones to serve as lookouts while they apply their art to walls. Drones may help some graffiti artists escape detection, but others have found themselves harboring much different opinions of drones. It seems police have discovered that drones can be very effective in catching graffiti artists at work.

In San Jose, California, police launched a drone in 2017 called the Graffiti Removal Automatic Drone, or GRAD. As GRAD patrols from above, it provides a video image to police. If the drone discovers graffiti artists at work, police on the ground are dispatched to the scene. Authorities say GRAD can be effective in swooping under bridges and into places that would ordinarily be hidden from view. "With this device, we will be able to get to those locations . . . and that will help us get ahead of the taggers," said San Jose mayor Sam Liccardo.

Authorities in Victoria, Australia, took the technology a step further in 2018 when they deployed drones equipped with heat sensors. That feature has enabled the drones to spot graffiti artists working at night. By working under cover of darkness, artists are often able to escape the video cameras mounted on drones, but these new heat-sensing drones pick up body heat, displaying hazy images of the artists at work. Police on the ground then respond to the locations identified by the drones. "These criminals are being watched," says Victoria detective Andrew Gustke.

Quoted in Vince Cestone, "Drones Are Latest Weapon in War on Graffiti in San Jose," KRON 4 News, September 13, 2017. www.kron4.com.

Quoted in Timna Jacks, "Metro Turns Up Heat on Paint-Can Vandals with Thermal-Imaging Drones," *Age*, September 24, 2018. www.theage.com.au.

see people arrested for illegally creating graffiti; rather, he hopes the law will help convince graffiti artists that the penalties are too harsh to risk getting caught painting a wall in the city. "I want this bill to be a deterrent," Todd says. "I don't want people to get fined, I want people to look at this fine and say, 'You know what? Putting this graffiti up isn't worth the potential that I'll get fined $2,500.'"[32]

Graffiti may now be a widely recognized form of art, but clearly the genre has never shaken its outlaw reputation. And many graffiti artists appear to have no interest in abiding by the law. Even though cities like Baltimore, Philadelphia, Austin, and Washington, DC, are willing to work with graffiti artists to keep their work within the confines of the law, many graffiti artists still prefer to work at night, tagging where they can, and now even using the technology of Google Earth and aerial drones to help them avoid detection.

CHAPTER FOUR

Creating a Following

Jim Clay Harper tags under the name Ether. Danielle Bremner's graffiti tag is Utah. They are a romantic and artistic tag team that has been painting graffiti together since they first met in 2005. The couple prefers to apply graffiti to subway cars and commuter trains, and in the past decade they have painted graffiti on the sides of trains around the globe—spray-painting trains in a total of thirty-seven cities in eleven countries. Harper says, "[The] metro system is really the heart of any given city. It's what connects the people to the city and to each other; it's how people move and get around and function throughout the day. I think there's something really special about going to a foreign place and being able to interact with the city and the people there in that kind of way."[33]

However, their mission to apply graffiti in international locations has been interrupted from time to time. In 2011 they were both arrested in New York City on vandalism charges and were sentenced to a year in jail. Upon their release from custody, the couple boarded a plane for India. They have never returned to the United States. Overseas, they have continued painting graffiti on trains, and the police have continued to pursue them. Once again, their mission was interrupted in 2016—this time in Melbourne, Australia, where Harper was caught painting graffiti on a storefront. Australian authorities sentenced Harper to six months in jail.

Their exploits and, in particular, their clashes with the law have led some to describe them as the Bonnie and Clyde of the graffiti world. The real Bonnie and Clyde were bank robbers Bonnie Parker and Clyde Barrow, whose exploits ended suddenly on May 23, 1934, when they were killed in a shootout with police. Years later, their love affair and engaging story led to numerous books published about their exploits as well as the production of the 1967 Academy Award–winning film, *Bonnie and Clyde.*

As with the real Bonnie and Clyde, this story of two young people in love, leading an outlaw life as graffiti artists, has captured the attention of fans around the world. Bremner and Harper have been willing participants in telling their story. They have made use of a number of Internet-based tools that have enabled the work of Utah and Ether to connect to a global audience.

Using Social Media

As Bremner and Harper create graffiti on trains, they often make videos of their work. In 2016 they produced a twelve-part video series titled *Probation Vacation: Lost in Asia*, and they uploaded the videos to the Vimeo and YouTube websites. The chapters show the couple applying graffiti to trains in cities in Turkey, India, Thailand, and other Asian nations. The films are well produced—sharply edited, with musical soundtracks, and often showing slices of everyday life filmed on city streets.

In each chapter, Bremner and Harper eventually make their way to a subterranean subway station or a remote railway yard where they film themselves applying bubble-lettered graffiti—freehand style—to subway cars. The couple obviously has had help producing the videos. Many of the scenes depict them climbing over fences or otherwise working together, which means somebody other than Bremner or Harper is holding the camera.

Some chapters in the series have received more than sixty-five thousand views on YouTube, but interest in the pair's exploits is believed to be much wider. Bremner and Harper post photos of their work on their Instagram account, which was reported to have more than 125,000 followers in 2018. They also have a Facebook page with some 25,000 followers, and they maintain a website. Bremner explains that "in a way, our work has nothing to do with social media, because everything we do is hand-made in the physical world. But in another sense, our work is tied into social media, as many people may not ever travel to the places we've been, and the way they connect with what we do is through something like Instagram."[34]

Enter the Invader

Bremner and Harper are not the only graffiti artists to make use of social media. Many artists have their own Instagram and Facebook accounts, and others submit photos of their work to social media pages established by individuals who invite anyone to provide submissions. By late 2018, some 35 million photos were tagged with the hashtag *graffiti* on Instagram. On Facebook, numerous pages are devoted to graffiti art, carrying names such as Graffiti, Graffiti Life, Graffiti Kings, Graffiti LifeStyle, Graffiti Kingdom, Graff Scene, and dozens more. Twitter accounts exist under names such as Graffiti Life, Street Art, Graffiti Kings, Graffiti Art Prog, and others.

> "Our work is tied into social media, as many people may not ever travel to the places we've been, and the way they connect with what we do is through something like Instagram."[34]
>
> —Graffiti artist Danielle Bremner

Many graffiti artists make use of social media to promote their work with an eye toward selling their art on canvas. Street artists who have transferred their art to canvas can easily—and often without cost—advertise their art on social media as well as across the wider Internet.

That is the strategy that has been employed successfully by a French graffiti artist who goes by the tag Invader. By late 2018, Invader's Instagram account, Invaderwashere, had more than 580,000 followers. As with many graffiti artists, he prefers not to reveal his true name. And when he poses for photographs, he always wears a mask depicting the comically mustached Salvador Dalí, the late Spanish surrealist painter. Although Invader remains a dedicat-

The French graffiti artist known as Invader produces works, made of ceramic tiles, that incorporate his personal "tag," which resembles an image from the 1970s video game Space Invaders.

ed street artist, he has also produced work for sale primarily using ceramic tiles in the style of his graffiti; in the process, he has become very wealthy. Some of his art has sold for as much as $300,000.

Promoting His Invasions

To help promote his work prior to a gallery opening, Invader visits the city where the show will be held and, for a period of a few months or more, spends nights in city neighborhoods tagging and bombing numerous walls. Fittingly, he refers to these city visits as invasions.

Invader's tag resembles a character from the 1970s-era video game *Space Invaders*. The artist has a great affinity for the block-style artwork of *Space Invaders* and similar video games from the era, and much of his street art is rendered in that style. After a few months of an invasion, he will likely have created hundreds of graffiti images on city walls and other exterior surfaces. During a 2018 invasion in Los Angeles, prior to the opening of his work at the city's Arts District gallery, he created about two hundred images around the city. In the meantime, he photographs

Graffiti Heading for Space

Graffiti artists have attracted attention beyond the art world. The European Space Agency (ESA), which oversees space missions for twenty-two European countries, looked for ways to get young people interested in space exploration. The agency came up with a space-themed graffiti art contest called Graffiti Without Gravity. The winner was to be given the opportunity to create the first street art in a weightless environment simulating space travel.

Working on canvas, artists were asked to create images promoting space travel. A dozen finalists were selected in May 2018. Two months later the finalists competed against one another, creating graffiti on canvas during a competition in the Dutch city of Noordwijk. Shane Sutton, a street artist from Dublin, Ireland, was ultimately declared the winner.

Sutton will be given the opportunity to create graffiti on canvas during the flights of the A320-Zero G, the aircraft employed by the ESA to help train astronauts for weightless flight. Based in Bordeaux, France, the aircraft flies in steep ascents and descents known as parabolas. Passengers aboard the aircraft are able to experience brief periods of weightlessness at the apex of each parabola. During those periods of weightlessness, Sutton will be invited to create art. According to a statement by the ESA, "He...will become the first street artist to make a piece of art in weightlessness. By means of a parabolic flight, this artist becomes the first street artist in [simulated] space."

European Space Agency, "Why Space and Art?," 2018. www.graffitiwithoutgravity.com.

all his artwork and creates maps showing the locations of his art, making the maps available on his website. In 2014 Invader even introduced a smartphone app that enables fans to photograph and store photos of his images. By using the app, his fans can compare images and score points for snapping the most Invader images. By late 2018, more than sixty-seven thousand users had downloaded the app.

Although Invader has certainly found a way to become an entrepreneur, the artist says he will never abandon graffiti. "Anybody can enjoy my work in the street, from the president to homeless people," he says. "My art has more visitors in the subways of New York than the Louvre [art museum in Paris]."[35]

Graffiti in the Galleries

Invader is not the first graffiti artist who has found ways to transform his or her street art into lucrative works on canvas or in other media. Nor is he alone in attracting the attention of private art collectors and winning praise from the mainstream art world. Andy Warhol and Jean-Michel Basquiat discovered back in the 1980s that many private collectors prize graffiti-inspired art.

Barry McGee, a graduate of the San Francisco Art Institute, has also built a following among art collectors and galleries. During the 1980s, McGee started creating street art on walls in San Francisco under the tag Twist. Since his street art days, though, McGee has made his art available as drawings and paintings, and has exhibited his work in numerous galleries. He is known for rendering colorful and comical faces as well as geometric shapes painted in psychedelic hues.

A visitor to the Carnegie Museum of Art in Pittsburgh, Pennsylvania, looks at a piece by artist Barry McGee, who is known for works that feature geometric figures painted in psychedelic hues.

For a 2013 exhibition at Boston's Institute of Contemporary Art, McGee produced his comical faces painted onto empty liquor bottles he found strewn around San Francisco. "Barry McGee is one of the most important contributors to the powerful and varied body of work that has emerged out of street culture," says Jill Medvedow, the institute's director. "His distinctive imagery, collaborative practice, and compassionate approach to the issues and energy of the streets have had a profound influence on a generation of artists."[36]

Graffiti Art in Museums

Many important street artists, among them Shepard Fairey and Banksy, have transferred their work to canvas, making their art available for sale in galleries. Moreover, Banksy, Fairey, and other graffiti artists have also found their work in demand by important art museums. These museums have staged exhibitions of graffiti-inspired art, thereby elevating street art to a plateau that has been occupied for centuries by oil paintings, watercolors, and sculpture.

One of the first museums to display a graffiti-related exhibition was the Museum of the City of New York. In 2014 the museum staged an exhibition titled *City as Canvas: Graffiti Art from the Martin Wong Collection*. Wong was an artist who painted gritty urban scenes on canvas, but he did not engage in street art. However, he appreciated the genre, and in 1989 he founded his own museum, the Museum of American Graffiti, displaying drawings, sketchbooks, and notes donated by a number of graffiti artists.

Wong closed the museum in 1994. He died in 1999, but before his death he donated his collection to the Museum of the City of New York. The 2014 exhibition displayed some 150 paintings, drawings, and photographs of street art in an exhibition space about the size of a basketball court. Says *New York Times* art critic Ken Johnson, "The exhibition's congestion works well as a reflection of graffiti's exuberant [recklessness]. It captures the communal spirit animating the artists, who . . . often collaborated, hung out together, competed with one another and collectively developed a kind of deliriously complicated [and] wild style."

Ken Johnson, "Writing Was on the Wall, and Some Still Remains," *New York Times*, February 7, 2014, p. C23.

Others in the art world share Medvedow's enthusiasm. McGee's artwork has been displayed in numerous galleries in the United States as well as in Japan, Italy, and Germany. Finding success in the mainstream art world has inspired a change in focus for McGee. Nowadays, he says, he mainly produces art for gallery shows. But an occasional tagging outing still has some appeal. "I did some tagging recently," he says, "but it was a special opportunity, so I took advantage of it. It's hard to explain, because it's automatic for me. . . . It felt good to do, though I worked anonymously, so no one would know that I did it."[37]

Preserving Their Work

Although street artists like Invader and McGee have found financial success and widespread followings, the vast number of graffiti artists will never achieve this degree of fame. Most will never see their work displayed in a gallery. Given the usual rush to clean walls of graffiti, many will not even see their work hours or days after they created it. They can, however, preserve their work online. And many have done just that. Some have created their own websites for this purpose or have posted images of their work on other sites. One website, the International Graffiti Archive (Intergraff), was established specifically to preserve images of outlaw graffiti. According to the website,

> We now know what we are looking for. . . . Strictly bombing, trains, rooftops, walls . . . you name it . . . all that stuff that will be buffed and painted over in the future has a little place in our hearts over here. Illegal graffiti is part of a diminishing culture that lacks the respect of anthropologists to really be examined and researched, and it probably won't be until it is all gone. Intergraff serves as a filter to collect every little piece of evidence to prove that graffiti once existed as a wild animal roaming in our sterile cities before everything is inevitably cleaned or painted over.[38]

The founders of Intergraff identify themselves as a group of artists and writers who are dedicated to preserving graffiti as an element of human culture. By 2018 some twenty-five thousand images of graffiti submitted by street artists in 146 cities from thirteen countries had been preserved on the site.

Street Art in Its Truest Form

Although organizations such as Intergraff are dedicated to preserving images created by street artists, not all graffiti artists are convinced that preserving street art on the Internet is necessarily a good thing. A graffiti artist known as Ces53—regarded

A passerby looks at graffiti in Prague, in the Czech Republic. Some graffiti artists oppose preserving their work on social media, instead urging people to get out and view their creations personally.

as a pioneer of street art in Denmark—urges people to look at graffiti online less and to get out into the streets where they can see it in its true and original form. He says, "The best graffiti experience is still the streets, to really see it with your own eyes, no iPhone can touch that, of course. I think that the so-called iPhone [and] Facebook hype is ridiculous and very impersonal anyway."[39]

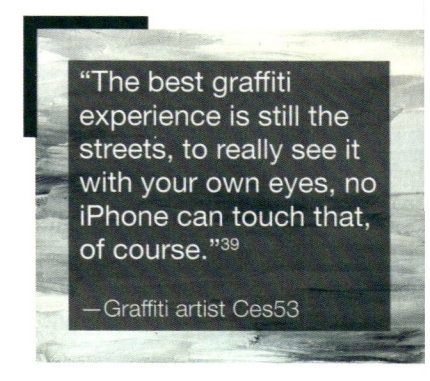

> "The best graffiti experience is still the streets, to really see it with your own eyes, no iPhone can touch that, of course."[39]
>
> —Graffiti artist Ces53

Artists like Ces53 believe graffiti should be appreciated in its truest form—on the street, created overnight by outlaw artists who carry on the traditions established decades ago by taggers like Cornbread and Taki 183. But there was no Internet when Cornbread and Taki 183 were tagging walls, which means virtually nobody outside their cities knew who they were. Today, street artists like Harper, Bremner, and Invader could not have achieved their fame without an online presence.

CHAPTER FIVE

The Messages of Graffiti

When college professor Christine Blasey Ford testified before the US Senate in 2018, accusing US Supreme Court nominee Brett Kavanaugh of sexually assaulting her when they were high school students during the 1980s, many women across America spoke up in support of her. Among Blasey Ford's strongest supporters were women in the street art community. In Philadelphia, graffiti artist Symone Salib created street art portraits of Blasey Ford and Anita Hill, who similarly testified before the Senate in 1991, alleging that she was sexually harassed by Supreme Court nominee Clarence Thomas. Salib created graffiti portraits of both women, each staring hard at passersby. Salib explains, "When you have a conversation with someone on a topic like that [sexual assault], they have an expression on their face that you won't forget."[40] Below the portraits of Blasey Ford and Hill, Salib painted the words "Believe Us." Surrounding the portraits of the two women, Salib painted smaller portraits of several members of the Senate, and below their portraits she wrote descriptions of them such as "weak," "conniving," "pushy," "lazy," and "bossy."

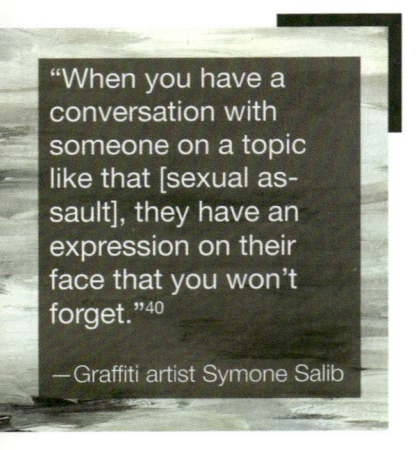

Explaining the motivation behind her work, Salib says, "A lot of the time, I'll hear something or see something or listen to a podcast. I'll find a story that resonates with me and I'm like, 'Wow, I

> "When you have a conversation with someone on a topic like that [sexual assault], they have an expression on their face that you won't forget."[40]
>
> —Graffiti artist Symone Salib

want everyone to hear this.' Anita Hill and Christine Blasey Ford's stories aren't that far off from other people's stories of sexual assault. We need to do better."[41]

Salib rendered the portraits of Blasey Ford and Hill on wheat paste, a technique used by many street artists. To paint the portraits, she first slathered an adhesive layer made of wheat flour and water onto the wall. The stencil art portraits were then painted atop the wheat paste layer in green and red paint.

Salib's work was true graffiti. She created the image on an exterior wall in the city without the owner's permission. To her surprise, the images of Blasey Ford and Hill remained on the wall for more than a month before the building owner removed them. In the meantime, a photograph of the Blasey Ford–Hill street art received nearly a thousand likes on Salib's Instagram account.

Artistic and Political Expression

Salib's work illustrates how graffiti artists often use street art to express their political views. Many graffiti artists prefer to be known as graffiti writers. They argue that their work is more than just visual—that it is meant to convey messages.

Using graffiti to express their political beliefs is a practice that has been exercised by street artists for decades. For example, about a century ago an anonymous graffiti writer protesting Great Britain's involvement in World War I scratched this inscription onto a wall of Richmond Castle in North Yorkshire, England: "You might as well try to dry a floor by throwing water on it as try to end this war by fighting."[42] At the time, the British government was using the castle as a prison for conscientious objectors—able-bodied British men who refused to report for military service. Therefore, it is likely the graffiti writer was a prisoner in the castle when he wrote his protest against the war. The graffiti writer's work was hardly artistic; nevertheless, he made his point.

In the past century, as graffiti has become more of an artistic expression, it has never lost its political themes. By the 1960s, the use of graffiti for both artistic and political expression exploded during the Cold War, the five-decade-long political conflict pitting the United States and its allies against the Soviet Union and its allies. The focal point of this conflict, and the prime location for the graffiti that accentuated the Cold War, was often the Berlin Wall.

At the close of World War II, the city of Berlin, Germany, was occupied by the United States, the United Kingdom, France, and the Soviet Union, which established separate zones to administer the city. By the early 1960s, the city remained split. It was administered on the western side by the freely elected German government and on the eastern side by a repressive German regime loyal to the Soviets. In 1961 the East German government erected a wall dividing the city.

The wall stood until 1989, when it was torn down as the Soviet Union and its allies in eastern Europe collapsed. But for the twenty-eight years of its existence, the Berlin Wall served as a grim symbol of the Cold War. It represented authoritarian barriers that prevented the peoples of East Germany and the other Soviet-dominated countries of Europe from enjoying the freedoms and democracy guaranteed to the West.

Graffiti on the Berlin Wall

Politically charged graffiti rarely found its way onto the eastern side of the Berlin Wall. Armed guards kept a stern watch over the wall, searching for Germans attempting to escape to the other side. This round-the-clock vigilance served also to persuade East German graffiti writers to keep their distance. But on the western side, the wall became a much-used canvas for personal and political expression. Berlin art curator Guillaume Trotin comments that

> the Berlin Wall also became the meeting point for the first generation of graffiti writers, some of them being the children of US servicemen, who brought the booming spirit of their local graffiti culture to West Berlin. . . . As the paintings

on the west side of the Wall flourished, the east side was left with the blank, sterile wall surface, where free artistic expression on the one side became a marker of social and cultural differences of separate societies.[43]

Among the images painted on the western side of the wall during the Cold War were comical portraits of Soviet leaders, renderings of the Statue of Liberty, images of American popular music stars, a winged angel flying over the wall, and prison bars with a handcuffed arm reaching out. In 1986 American graffiti artist Keith

A winged angel flying over the Berlin Wall was among a number of images that graffiti artists in West Berlin painted.

Haring showed up at the wall and painted one of his cartoonish characters writhing in agony. After painting the graffiti, Haring told a reporter the meaning of his image: "It's about the ridiculousness of all walls and enemies and borders. . . . [The graffiti is a] humanistic gesture, more than anything else. [It's] a political and subversive act—an attempt to psychologically destroy the wall by painting it."[44]

Graffiti in North Korea

The regime that rules the nation of North Korea is one of the most repressive governments in the world. Free speech is not protected. Dissent is not tolerated. Citizens charged with speaking out against the regime of North Korean leader Kim Jong-un are usually sentenced to lengthy prison terms or even executed.

Faced with such terrible consequences, North Korea's graffiti artists nevertheless apply street art to walls in the North Korean capital of Pyongyang whenever they can, speaking out against the regime. One recent graffiti message read, "Punish Kim Jong-un, the enemy of the people." Elsewhere, graffiti at construction sites has mocked government slogans urging laborers to work harder.

In response, the regime has taken some unusual steps to crack down on graffiti. In 2018, for example, the government ordered North Korean citizens to provide handwriting samples in an effort to match the handwriting of the culprits who painted city walls. Some twenty thousand North Koreans are believed to have provided handwriting samples to police.

Following the handwriting tests, two individuals were arrested—one of whom was a colonel serving in the North Korean military. The colonel and his alleged accomplice were executed by a firing squad in May 2018 and their families were thrown into prison camps. One North Korean official stated that they "had reportedly defaced many buildings with graffiti criticizing Kim's regime over the past three years."

Quoted in Elizabeth Shim, "Report: North Korea on Alert After Anti-Kim Jong Un Flyers Found," United Press International, December 13, 2016. www.upi.com.

Quoted in Jay Akbar, "Writing's on the Wall: Kim Jong-un Executed a Top Colonel and His Accomplice for Writing Graffiti Slamming the North Korean Tyrant's Leadership," *Sun*, May 22, 2018. www.thesun.co.uk.

Graffiti on the West Bank Wall

In the years since the Berlin Wall was torn down, other walls have been erected along national borders, and they, too, have emerged as the focal points of international conflicts. One of those walls separates the nation of Israel from the contested region of the Middle East known as the West Bank. In 1967 war erupted between Israel and three Arab nations: Egypt, Jordan, and Syria. The war was brief, lasting a mere six days and resulting in an overwhelming victory for the Israelis. At the conclusion of the conflict, Israel seized Arab land along its borders to help ensure the country's security, including a 2,100-square-mile (5,500 sq km) territory known as the West Bank.

In the years since the war, the region has evolved into a political tinderbox as Palestinian Arabs have claimed the West Bank as part of their homeland. Often, the region has fallen into war and terrorism. In 2002 the Israeli government began construction of a 443-mile (712 km) wall separating Israel from the West Bank. By 2018 the wall was still under construction, with about 65 percent of the structure completed.

As the Israelis erected the wall, graffiti artists on both sides followed the construction crews, applying politically charged street art to the concrete. On the Palestinian side of the wall, artists paint symbols of the Islamic faith; the Dome of the Rock, an Islamic shrine in the Israeli city of Jerusalem, is often depicted. Artists also paint natural themes, and the sabra cactus is often depicted. The sabra cactus is regarded by Palestinians as a symbol of their struggle. The sabra is a prickly cactus, known to survive in the harshest conditions, and it is also known to grow back when cut down. Another image painted repeatedly on the wall is a portrait of a young Palestinian boy known as Handala. The original image of Handala was created by Naji al-Ali, a Palestinian cartoonist. According to Christine Leuenberger, a sociologist at Cornell University in Ithaca, New York, "For Palestinians, the famous image created by Palestinian cartoonist Naji al-Ali

A wall separating Israeli and Palestinian territory is the site of graffiti featuring politically charged messages.

symbolizes their suffering and a long wait for justice. Handala usually has his back turned and his hands clasped behind his back. The story tells us that he will not turn around until justice comes to Palestine."[45]

Unlike the Berlin Wall, though, where the vigilant East German police maintained a sharp eye for subversives, the Israeli side of the West Bank wall is also filled with politically charged graffiti. Many Israelis are sympathetic to the plight of the Palestinians and have called on the Israeli government to tear down the wall and turn the West Bank over to the Palestinians as part of their homeland. US president Donald Trump, who supports the West Bank wall and construction of a wall on the US-Mexico border, has emerged as a favorite target, and many graffiti artists have painted comical depictions of him. Moreover, in 2017 Banksy made a secret visit to the wall, painting nine surrealist stencil art images on the Israeli side. One image of note showed a young girl forcing a soldier to stand with his hands against the wall while she searched him for weapons. Observers believe Banksy's art has been responsible for drawing scores of tourists to the wall each day, helping generate sympathy for the Palestinians' cause.

> "Handala usually has his back turned and his hands clasped behind his back. The story tells us that he will not turn around until justice comes to Palestine."[45]
>
> —Cornell University sociologist Christine Leuenberger

Graffiti and Free Speech

In the United States, graffiti has usually been viewed as either vandalism or art. Some argue that it should also be regarded as constitutionally protected free speech. Under the US Constitution, free speech is protected by the First Amendment. In other words, the right of Americans to publicly express their opinions is guaranteed under federal law. In the case of graffiti, though, courts and constitutional scholars agree that if the street art has been rendered illegally, it is not protected by the First Amendment. Communities have established laws protecting the rights of property owners, and if their rights are infringed on by outlaw graffiti artists, they have every right to have the graffiti removed, whatever the messages contained in the graffiti may be. These laws, therefore, do not address the messages of the graffiti, only that it may have been painted in violation of the rights of the property owner.

But graffiti painted with the permission of the property owner offers a different side to the story. In Portland, Maine, the city government permits graffiti artists to create art on a 100-foot (30 m) wall that is located on property owned by the city's water department. In 2016, though, a portrait of Maine's governor, Paul LePage, appeared on the wall. The graffiti artist rendered LePage wearing the hood and robes of the Ku Klux Klan (KKK)—a group whose racist activities date back to the post–Civil War period.

The image appeared on the wall shortly after LePage was quoted in the press complaining about illegal immigration to the United States by people from Latin American countries. He said, "You try to identify the enemy and the enemy right now, the overwhelming majority of people coming in, are people of color or people of Hispanic origin."[46] The anonymous graffiti artist who painted the image of LePage seemed to be reacting to the governor's statement, which the artist found to be of a racist nature.

In Portland, city officials said they wanted the graffiti portrait of LePage removed. "I do not want it up there; it is not reflective of our values," said Portland mayor Ethan Strimling. "The KKK has a long, problematic history in the state of Maine and equating the governor and his rhetoric, as much as we disagree with it, is a step too far."[47]

When graffiti mocking the state's governor appeared on a public art space in Portland, Maine, outraged city officials ordered that it be removed, while the city's attorneys argued that the image constituted free speech and was therefore protected.

Graffiti and Hate Speech

When rendered with the property owner's permission, the US Constitution protects graffiti as free speech—but not if the artist uses a public space to attack people's ethnicities or faiths. And although graffiti painted without permission is illegal on those grounds alone, hate-filled graffiti is regarded as a separate, and far more serious, offense. In the United States, federal and state governments have declared such graffiti to be hate crimes. In most cases, artists caught painting walls with hate-filled graffiti, with or without the permission of the owners, are often sentenced to lengthy jail terms.

On August 22, 2017, after a night of excessive drinking and drug use, George Rissell painted several racist messages, as well as the Nazi symbol of the swastika, on several buildings and cars in the Philadelphia suburb of Coatesville. The swastika is considered to be a hate-filled symbol targeting Jews. He was caught in the act by police, who then arrested and charged him with committing hate crimes. Had Rissell simply painted common graffiti that night, he probably would have faced no more than a fine and term of probation. But since his graffiti was racially and ethnically motivated, he was sentenced to a prison term of seven to fourteen years. In sentencing Rissell, Judge Patrick Carmody said, "Being drunk, that doesn't excuse being racist. You're both trying to scare [people] and you're trying to incite violence."

Quoted in Erin McCarthy, "Coatesville Man Sentenced to State Prison for Racist, Anti-Semitic Graffiti," *Philadelphia Inquirer*, June 27, 2018. www.philly.com.

"Provocative Art"

But the city's water department did not immediately carry out the mayor's demands. Officials of the water department consulted city attorneys, who concluded that the portrait of LePage had been painted on a wall approved for graffiti and, therefore, the artist's portrait of the governor had to be regarded as constitutionally protected free speech. Alison Beyea, the executive director of the Maine branch of the American Civil Liberties Union, which often provides legal assistance in free speech cases, stresses that "in a free society, individuals decide what opinions and beliefs they want to see—not the government. Provocative art can test our dedication to this belief, but that is exactly why we have the Constitution to guide us."[48]

As things turned out, the depiction of LePage as a KKK member only stayed on the wall a short time. While the debate over free speech raged at Portland City Hall, another graffiti artist doctored the LePage portrait. The artist painted over the KKK hood and robes, replacing them with huge black, round ears, giving the governor something of a resemblance to the cartoon character Mickey Mouse—obviously, an attempt to make the governor look more like a clownish oaf than a racist.

Whether the graffiti artists chose to portray LePage as a racist or merely a clown, there is no question that the intents of the artists were politically charged. As graffiti continues to dominate twenty-first-century culture, it is likely that politically motivated art will continue to find a home on public walls, subway cars, and other outdoor surfaces in free societies. After all, graffiti artists have been tagging walls since prehistoric times, and future artists will likely be inclined to make their very public and provocative creations available to society.

Source Notes

Introduction: Art That Is Hard to Miss

1. Quoted in Lucy Guanuna, "Getting Up, Staying Up: History of Graffiti in the LA River," KCET, September 17, 2015. www.kcet.org.
2. George C. Stowers, "Graffiti Art: An Essay Concerning the Recognition of Some Forms of Graffiti as Art," Art Crimes, 1997. www.graffiti.org.
3. Quoted in Edward A. Brown, "Is Graffiti Art?," *BU Today*, Boston University, March 2, 2009. www.bu.edu.
4. Vivien Raynor, "Art: Basquiat, Warhol," *New York Times*, September 20, 1985, p. C22.
5. Gagosian Gallery, "Jean-Michel Basquiat and Andy Warhol: Olympic Rings," 2018. https://gagosian.com.

Chapter One: The History of Graffiti

6. R. Dale Guthrie, *The Nature of Paleolithic Art*. Chicago: University of Chicago Press, 2005, p. 141.
7. Bill Norrington, "The Geography of Graffiti," Department of Geography, University of California, Santa Barbara, 2018. https://geog.ucsb.edu.
8. Quoted in Hagia Sophia Museum, "Viking Scripture in Hagia Sophia," 2018. http://ayasofyamuzesi.gov.tr.
9. Paul Dickson, *War Slang: American Fighting Words and Phrases Since the Civil War*. Mineola, NY: Dover, 2011, p. 182.
10. Quoted in Roger Gastman and Caleb Neelon, *The History of American Graffiti*. New York: Harper Design, 2010, p. 50.
11. Quoted in Valerie Russ, "Off the Wall: Cornbread and Other Early Graffiti Writers Speak," *Philadelphia Inquirer*, June 25, 2016. www2.philly.com.

12. Quoted in Gastman and Neelon, *The History of American Graffiti*, p. 56.
13. James Farina, "Top 3 Benefits of Stencil Graffiti Art," 2018. http://stencilgraffitiart.com.
14. Quoted in Brown, "Is Graffiti Art?"
15. Quoted in Angie Crouch, "'The World Is Our Canvas': Nonprofit Empowers Street Artists to Uplift Neighborhoods," NBC Los Angeles, February 12, 2017. www.nbclosangeles.com.
16. Quoted in Jareen Imam, "From Graffiti to Galleries: Street vs. Public Art," CNN, August 5, 2012. www.cnn.com.

Chapter Two: Graffiti Artists of Influence

17. Quoted in Kobi Annobil, "Shepard Fairey," *Format*, January 21, 2008. http://formatmag.com.
18. Quoted in Annobil, "Shepard Fairey."
19. Quoted in Haring Foundation, "Pop Shop," 2018. www.haring.com.
20. Quoted in Arthur Lubow, "It's Going to Be Big," *Inc.*, March 1, 2009. www.inc.com.
21. Quoted in Henry Chalfant and Sacha Jenkins, *Training Days: The Subway Artists Then and Now*. New York: Thames and Hudson, 2014, p. 93.
22. Jasmin Hernandez, "Graffiti Queen Lady Pink Still Reigns Supreme," Vice, July 28, 2016. www.vice.com.
23. Quoted in Marissa Payne, "Take a Look at What Artist Duo 'Os Gemeos' Did to Brazil's World Cup Soccer Team Plane," *Washington Post*, May 28, 2014. www.washingtonpost.com.
24. *Find*, "Art: An Analysis of Banksy," May 21, 2010. https://thefindmag.com.

Chapter Three: Emerging from the Underground

25. Quoted in Complex, "The 50 Biggest Street Art Arrests," April 25, 2012. www.complex.com.

26. Quoted in Sarah Booker-Lewis, "Instagram and Snapchat Blamed for Increase in Graffiti," *Brighton and Hove News*, November 19, 2018. www.brightonandhovenews.org.
27. Deborah L. Weisel, *Graffiti*, US Justice Department, May 2009. www.ncjrs.gov.
28. Patricia D. Ziegler, "When Being 'Tagged' Is Not a Game," *Coatings Tech*, August 2014, p. 6.
29. Quoted in Wil Crisp, "Social Media Is Fuelling a Surge in Rail Graffiti," *Telegraph*, May 5, 2018. www.telegraph.co.uk.
30. Eric A. Vasallo, "The Evolution of Street Art," Medium, April 2, 2016. https://medium.com.
31. Quoted in Fox 5, "Artists Helping Brighten and Revitalize DC Neighborhoods as Part of MuralsDC Project," October 5, 2018. www.fox5dc.com.
32. Quoted in Jessica Contrera, "Washington Is Fighting Graffiti Artists—but It Loves the Graffiti Aesthetic," *Washington Post*, March 22, 2016. www.washingtonpost.com.

Chapter Four: Creating a Following

33. Quoted in Sami Emory, "Renegade Graffiti Artists Utah & Ether Aren't Afraid of Getting Caught," Vice, November 6, 2016. https://creators.vice.com.
34. Quoted in Emory, "Renegade Graffiti Artists Utah & Ether Aren't Afraid of Getting Caught."
35. Quoted in Deborah Vankin, "French Street Artist Invader Heads 'Into the White Cube' for a Solo Show—and into the Streets for a New L.A. 'Invasion,'" *Los Angeles Times*, November 15, 2018. www.latimes.com.
36. Quoted in Miriam M. Barnum, "From Graffiti to Gallery," *Harvard Crimson*, April 17, 2013. www.thecrimson.com.
37. Quoted in Paul Laster, "Graffiti Artist Barry McGee Brings Streets Smarts to His Latest Gallery Show," Time Out, January 8, 2018. www.timeout.com.
38. International Graffiti Archive, "Mission," 2010. http://intergraff.com.

39. Quoted in ILoveGraffiti, "Interview—Ces53," 2013. http://ilovegraffiti.de.

Chapter Five: The Messages of Graffiti

40. Quoted in Bethany Ao, "Female Street Artists Invoke Political Themes," *Philadelphia Inquirer*, November 6, 2018, p. C6.
41. Quoted in Ao, "Female Street Artists Invoke Political Themes," p. C6.
42. Quoted in Joshua Kelly, "This 100-Year-Old Antiwar Graffiti Is Going to Be Saved," Public Radio International, May 17, 2016. www.pri.org.
43. Guillaume Trotin, "Berlin Street Art History—Where Graffiti Found Home," Berlin Street Art, February 24, 2016. https://berlinstreetart.com.
44. Quoted in Allison McNearney, "When Keith Haring Graffitied the Berlin Wall," Daily Beast, April 29, 2017. www.thedailybeast.com.
45. Christine Leuenberger, "The West Bank Wall as Canvas: Art and Graffiti in Palestine/Israel," *Palestine-Israel Journal*, November 12, 2011. www.pij.org.
46. Quoted in Amber Phillips, "LePage Doubles Down: 'The Enemy Right Now' Is 'People of Color or People of Hispanic Origin,'" *Washington Post*, August 27, 2016. www.washingtonpost.com.
47. Quoted in Sarah Larimer, "Mural Depicting Gov. Paul LePage in KKK Regalia Sparks Painting Fight in Maine's Biggest City," *Washington Post*, September 7, 2016. www.washingtonpost.com.
48. Quoted in Peter McGuire, "Scathing LePage Mural Tests Portland's Stance on Free Speech," *Portland Press Herald*, September 6, 2016. www.pressherald.com.

For Further Research

Books

Lou Chamberlin, *Street Art: International*. Richmond, Australia: Hardie Grant, 2016.

Jurgen Doring and Claus Von Der Osten, eds., *Keith Haring: Posters*. London: Prestel, 2017.

Tyson Mitman, *The Art of Defiance: Graffiti, Politics and the Reimagined City in Philadelphia*. Chicago: Intellect, 2018.

Chloé Ragazzoli et al., eds., *Scribbling Through History: Graffiti, Places and People from Antiquity to Modernity*. London: Bloomsbury Academic, 2018.

Lori Zimmer, *The Art of Spray Paint: Inspirations and Techniques from Masters of Aerosol*. Beverly, MA: Quarto, 2017.

Internet Sources

Sami Emory, "Renegade Graffiti Artists Utah & Ether Aren't Afraid of Getting Caught," Vice, November 6, 2016. https://creators.vice.com.

Jasmin Hernandez, "Graffiti Queen Lady Pink Still Reigns Supreme," Vice, July 28, 2016. www.vice.com.

Valerie Russ, "Off the Wall: Cornbread and Other Early Graffiti Writers Speak," *Philadelphia Inquirer*, June 25, 2016. www2.philly.com.

Guillaume Trotin, "Berlin Street Art History—Where Graffiti Found Home," Berlin Street Art, February 24, 2016. https://berlinstreetart.com.

Eric A. Vasallo, "The Evolution of Street Art," Medium, April 2, 2016. https://medium.com.

Websites

Art Crimes (www.graffiti.org). Sponsored by a group of graffiti enthusiasts, this website has gathered numerous articles about street art as well as thousands of photos of graffiti. Each month the site highlights the work of a dozen or more graffiti artists. Visitors can click on the tags of each artist to review their work. A search engine enables visitors to find interviews with street artists as well as other news articles about graffiti.

Beautify Earth (https://beautifyearth.org). Located in Santa Monica, California, this organization sponsors legal street art projects. Its website includes interviews with artists who work in the program and examples of their art. The site also includes videos of street artists at work on Beautify Earth projects.

International Graffiti Archive (http://intergraff.com). The archive is dedicated to preserving the work of graffiti artists around the globe. By 2018 some twenty-five thousand images had been uploaded to the site. By following the "Archive" link, visitors can find databases for individual countries and cities, giving them access to photos of street art.

Keith Haring Foundation (http://haring.com). This nonprofit foundation is dedicated to preserving the work of Keith Haring. Its website includes an archive of the late street artist's work, including sketchbooks, essays written by Haring, his press interviews, maps showing the locations of murals painted by Haring, and updates on new exhibitions of Haring's work.

Utah and Ether (http://utahether.com). This website chronicles the exploits of the outlaw graffiti artists Danielle Bremner and Jim Clay Harper, who tag under the names Utah and Ether and occasionally find themselves in police custody. By following the "Work" link, visitors can view the site's "Moments in Crime" page, which features photos of Bremner and Harper painting graffiti on trains.

Index

Note: Boldface page numbers indicate illustrations.

aerial drones, 37, 44
airplanes, 30
Ali, Naji al-, 61–62
Andre the Giant Has A Posse stickers, 21–22
Apollinaire, Guillaume, 32
artists
  freehand, 16
  influential
    Banksy, 21, 26, 30–32, **31**, 63
    Ecko (Milecofsky), 21, 25–27
    Fabara (Lady Pink), 21, 27–29
    Fairey, 21–23, 43
    Haring, 21, 23–25, **24**, 59–60
    Pandolfo brothers (OSGEMEOS), 21, **29**, 29–30
  motivation, 15, 16
    See also political expression
  stencil, **15**, 16–18
  tech aid for, 37
  use of pseudonyms by, 14
Austin, 42–43
Australia, **38**, 41, 44

Ayad, Vic, 42–43

Baltimore Mural Program, 40
Banksy, 21, 26, 30–32, **31**, 63
Barrow, Clyde, 46–47
Basquiat, Jean-Michel, 8–9
Beautify Earth (Santa Monica, California), 18–19
Berlin Wall, 58–60, **59**
Bethlehem, Pennsylvania, 43
Beyea, Alison, 65–66
Blasey Ford, Christine, 56, 57
Blek le Rat, 17–18
Blondie, 8
bombing, defined, 17
Bonnie and Clyde (film), 47
"Borderline" (song), 8
Boston, 52
Bremner, Danielle (Utah), 46–48
Brooklyn Museum (New York City), 29
bubble letters, defined, 17
"Buffalo Gal" (song), 8
burner, defined, 17

Carmody, Patrick, 65
Carnegie Museum of Art (Pittsburgh), **51**
Carr, Carolyn, 23
Carson Creek Ranch, 43
Ces53, 54–55

characteristics
  created at night, 6
  has properties of art, 7
  locations, 8
Cheatham, Andi Scull, 42–43
City as Canvas: Graffiti Art from the Martin Wong Collection (exhibition), 52
Coatings Tech (industry trade magazine), 36–37
computer applications, 37
construction materials, 35, 36–37
contests, 50
Cornbread, 14–15
Cortesão, Luísa, 12
crazy, defined, 17
Crush Walls (Denver, Colorado), 18–19

Dickson, Paul, 13
drones, 37, 44
Durham, Ontario (Canada), 41

Ecko, Marc (Milecofsky), 21, 25–27
Ecko Unlimited, 27
Einstein graffiti mural, 40
Ether (Harper), 46–48
European Space Agency (ESA), 50

Fabara, Sandra (Lady Pink), 21, 27–29
Facebook, graffiti art on, 47–48

Fairey, Shepard, 21–23, 43
Farina, James, 16
Fekner, John, 16–17
Find (magazine), 32
First Amendment right, graffiti as, 63–66, **64**
Free, Steven, 34–35
free speech, graffiti as, 63–66, **64**

Gagosian Gallery (London, England), 9
gangs, 7–8, 13
Girafa, 34–35
Girl with a Balloon (Banksy), 26
Goring, Jeff, 41
graffiti, origin of term, 6
Graffiti HeART (Cleveland, Ohio), 18–19
Graffiti Removal Automatic Drone (GRAD), 44
Graffiti Without Gravity contest, 50
Great Britain, cost of removal in, 35
Groninger Museum (Netherlands), 29
Gustke, Andrew, 44
Guthrie, R. Dale, 10

Hagia Sophia (Istanbul, Turkey), 12
Halvdan, 12
Handala, 61–62
"Hardest Part, The" (song), 8

Haring, Keith, 21, 23–25, **24**, 59–60
Harper, Jim Clay (Ether), 46–48
Harry, Debbie, 8
hate speech, 65
Hernandez, Jasmin, 28
High School of Art and Design (New York City), 28
Hill, Anita, 56, 57
history
  birthplace of modern, 14–15
  early New York City graffiti, 15–17
  gangs, 7–8
  "Kilroy Was Here," 13
  music videos, 8
  Paleolithic art, 10, **11**
  Roman, 11
  Viking, 11–12
  Warhol-Basquiat exhibit, 8–9
Hope Outdoor Gallery, 42–43

Instagram, 47, 48, 57
Institute of Contemporary Art (Boston), 52
International Graffiti Archive (Intergraff, website), 53–54
Invader, 48–50, **49**

Jahanbin, Nessar, 39–40
Johnson, Ken, 52

Kilroy, James J., 12–13
Kilroy drawing, 13
Kool Klepto Kidd, 14

Lady Pink (Fabara), 21, 27–29
Lakewood Airport (New Jersey), 25
Lascaux caves (France), 10, **11**
LATA 65, 12
laws
  building owners as responsible for removal, 43
  graffiti as vandalism, 34–35
  hate speech, 65
  penalties
    fines, 35, 43, 44
    jail sentences, 43, 44, 46
    quality of life and perceptions of public safety, 36
legal graffiti, **38**
  Austin, 42–43
  Baltimore Mural program, 40
  Mural Arts Philadelphia program, 40–42, **42**
  MuralsDC program, 38–40
  Sydney, Australia, **38**, 41
legitimacy, proof of, 18–19, 20
LePage, Paul, 63–66, **64**
Liccardo, Sam, 44
Lisbon (Portugal), 12
Living Walls (Atlanta, Georgia), 18–19
Los Angeles County Museum of Art, 23
Los Angeles River, 6, **7**

Madonna, 8
materials and techniques, 20
  freehand, 15–16

paint, markers, pencils, 13–14
stencils, 12, **15**, 16–17
wheat paste, 57
McCray, Daryl, 14–15
McGee, Barry (Twist), **51**, 51–53
McLaren, Malcolm, 8
Medvedow, Jill, 52
Melbourne, Australia, 46
Metropolitan Museum of Art (New York City), 29
Meyer, Evan, 19
Milecofsky, Marc (Ecko), 21, 25–27
Milecofsky, Marci, 27
Mitchell, Gill, 35
Mural Arts Philadelphia program, 40–42, **42**
murals, **19**, **38**
  Austin, 42–43
  Australia, **38**, 41
  Baltimore, 40
  Banksy, 32
  Fabara, 28
  Fairey, 23
  graffiti compared to, 19–20
  Mural Arts Philadelphia program, 40–42, **42**
  MuralsDC, 38–40
  OSGEMEOS, 30
museum exhibits
  in Boston, 52
  in England, 23
  in Los Angeles, 23
  in Netherlands, 29
  in New York City, 29, 52
  in Pittsburgh, **51**
  in Washington, DC, 23
Museum of American Graffiti, 52
Museum of the City of New York, 52
music videos, graffiti as backdrop for, 8

National Portrait Gallery (Washington, DC), 23
Netherlands, 29
Newtown, Australia, 41
New York City
  arrests for graffiti, 46
  early graffiti in, 15–17
  museums, 29, 52
  Pop Shop, 25
  schools, 18, 28
  Seward Park High School, 18
  on subways, 23–24, 28
New York Times (newspaper), 8–9, 15, 52
nonprofit organizations, promoting graffiti-style art, 18–19
Norrington, Bill, 11
North Korea, 60

Obama, Barack, Fairey poster of, 23
O'Donnell, Hugh, 8, 18

Off the Wall (Sherman Oaks, California), 18–19
OSGEMEOS (Gustavo and Otavio Pandolfo), 21, **29**, 29–30

Pabst, Greville, 41
Paleolithic art, 10, **11**
Pandolfo, Gustavo and Otavio (OSGEMEOS), 21, **29**, 29–30
Paris, France, 17–18
Parker, Bonnie, 46–47
Philadelphia, 14–15, 40–42, **42**
political expression
  in North Korea, 60
  opposing
    sexual harassment, 56–57
    urban blight, 17
    war, 57
  on West Bank Wall, 61–63, **62**
  on west side of Berlin Wall, 58–60, **59**
Pompeii (Roman city), 11
Pop Shop (New York City), 25
Portland, Maine, 63–66, **64**
Portugal, legal graffiti in, 12
power-washing, 35
Prague, Czech Republic, **54**
Probation Vacation: Lost in Asia (video series), 47
Prou, Xavier, 17–18

Queen Matilda (Fabara), 28–29

rat image, 17–18
Raynor, Vivien, 8–9
removal, **36**
  building owners as responsible for, 43
  cost of, 35, 43–45
  techniques, 35
Rhode Island School of Design, 21
Rissell, George, 65
Rodrigues, Lara, 12
Rome, ancient, 11
Rushmore, R.J., 26

sales of works on canvas, 48–49
Salib, Symone, 56–57
sandblasting, 35
San Jose, California, 44
Seward Park High School (New York City), 18
Site-Specific Art (Boston University course), 18
Skrederstu, Evan, 6
Smithsonian Institution (Washington, DC), 23
social media, 47–48
Sotheby's auction, 26
spray paint, 13–14
stencil artists, **15**, 16–18, 21–23
sticker, defined, 17
Stone Age art, 10, **11**
Stowers, George C., 6–7
street art, 6

77

Strimling, Ethan, 64
subways, tagging on
  exposure as reason for, 46, 50
  filming, 47–48
  in New York City, 23–24, 28
surrealism, 32
Sutton, Shane, 50
Sydney, Australia, **38**

tags and tagging, 17, 20
  See also subways, tagging on
Taki 183, 15–16
terms, 6, 17
Time (magazine), 31–32
Todd, Brandon T., 43–45
Trotin, Guillaume, 58–59
Trump, Donald, 62
Tucillo, Gino, 20
Twist (McGee), **51**, 51–53
Twitter, 48

Urban Artworks (Seattle, Washington), 18–19
Utah (Bremner), 46–48

vandalism, graffiti as, 34–35
  building owners as responsible for removal, 43
  penalties, 35, 43, 44, 46
  quality of life and perceptions of public safety, 36
Vasallo, Eric A., 39
Vice (website), 28
Victoria, Australia, 44
Victoria and Albert Museum (London, England), 23
Viking graffiti, 11–12
Vikings, 11–12

Warhol, Andy, 8–9
Washington, DC
  MuralsDC program, 38–40
  museums, 23
  removal costs and fines, 43–45
website for graffiti, 53–54
West Bank Wall, 61–63, **62**
Whitney Museum (New York City), 29
Wong, Martin, 52

Ziegler, Patricia D., 36–37

Picture Credits

Cover: Visun Khankasem/Shutterstock.com

7: Associated Press
11: thipjang/Shutterstock.com
15: Richard E. Levine/Newscom
19: Leonard Zhukovsky/Shutterstock.com
24: Tuttomondo, The Last Public Keith Haring Performance/ Photo ©Marcello Mencarini/Bridgeman Images
29: Chico A. Ferreira/picture-alliance/dpa/AP Images
31: Associated Press
36: Britta Pedersen/picture-alliance/dpa/AP Images
38: Hugh Peterswald/Sipa USA/Newscom
42: Associated Press
49: Mark Baker/ZUMA Press/Newscom
51: Associated Press
54: emka74/Shuttertock.com
59: Berlin Wall Memorial/Photo ©Paule Saviano/Bridgeman Images
62: Zoriah/ZUMA Press/Newscom
64: Associated Press

About the Author

Hal Marcovitz is a former newspaper reporter and columnist. He has written nearly two hundred books for young readers. His other book in the Art Scene series is *The Art of Tattoos*. He makes his home in Chalfont, Pennsylvania.